Christmas

by
Carrie Clane

Christmas in Killarney

Copyright © 2022 Carrie Clane.

All rights reserved. No part of this publication may be reproduced, distributed, or transmitted in any form or by any means, including photocopying, recording, or other electronic or mechanical methods, without the prior written permission of the publisher, except in the case of brief quotations embodied in critical reviews and certain other non-commercial uses permitted by copyright law.

For permissions and media enquiries please visit
https://carrieclane.wixsite.com/contact

ISBN: 979-8-35615648-9 (Paperback)
ISBN: 979-8-86156900-2 (Hardcover)

This is a work of fiction. Names, characters, organisations, places, events, and incidents are either products of the author's imagination or are used fictitiously. Any resemblance to actual persons, living or dead, or actual events, is purely coincidental.

Front cover design Copyright © 2022 Shane Braddish.

Cover image "Traditional Irish cottage at winter time - Adare Co. Limerick" by Kwiatek7, licensed for commercial use courtesy of Shutterstock.

Cover image "Christmas Wreath" by Marigold_88, licensed for commercial use courtesy of Depositphotos.

"Christmas Wish Calligraphy" Font by Roland Huse Design, licensed for commercial use courtesy of Creative Fabrica B.V.

Vectors & clipart licensed for commercial use courtesy of Shutterstock, Depositphotos and Creative Fabrica B.V.

Amazon and the Amazon logo, are trademarks of Amazon.com, Inc., or its affiliates.

For Cherie and Noel
Banzai

Chapter 1

Not even the first snowfall of the holiday season could deter the hardy New Yorkers from queuing outside Madison Square Gardens for the big event. Most of them had been fans of Kade since she'd first burst onto the scene as a fresh faced 14 year old with her debut multi-platinum selling album. Now, almost 16 years later, they were still coming in their thousands to hear her sing and tonight was a special occasion for all of them. For the last two years, Kade had been off on her wildly successful world tour, selling out stadiums from Rio de Janeiro to Tokyo, but now she was back in her hometown to kick off the North American leg of her tour with a show that had been sold out for months in advance. From hard-core fans who'd been there from the very beginning to young boys and girls being chaperoned to their first ever concert, the mix of people from different backgrounds and walks of life was a testament to how Kade had reached out across the boundaries to appeal to everyone and so it came as no surprise to see the fashion designers of Soho chatting excitedly with bus drivers from Bed-Stuy as they waited for the doors to open.

It seemed like every reporter in the country had turned up to cover the show and from under the giant Christmas tree in front of the Garden they broadcast to the world. In spite of the biting cold, an intrepid TV reporter was braving the elements to deliver her live report for the evening news.

"This is AJ, coming to you from New York where Kade kicks off her homecoming tour in style with a Christmas spectacular that promises to be one of her biggest and best yet."

As AJ spoke, a limo pulled up to the VIP entrance behind her and when a handsome young man in his early twenties stepped out onto the red carpet the crowd went wild. Sensing a scoop, AJ ditched her prepared script and rushed over with her cameraman to see if she could snatch a quick interview with the new arrival.

"And look who's just shown up viewers, it's Kade's boyfriend, movie star Matty Brown."

Matty was busy signing autographs for the adoring crowd but quickly broke off when he saw the TV cameras approaching.

"So Matty, you must be really excited?" Asked AJ, thrusting the microphone in his direction.

"I sure am," replied Matty as he turned on the charm for the camera, "My new movie drops in four days' time."

"I meant about the concert?" AJ clarified.

"Oh yeah, that too," said Matty, quickly glossing over the subject. "I play Balthazar, the ghost of a seventeenth century vampire who falls in love with a zombie TikToker," he continued, "It's called Everlasting Love."

"And how is Kade feeling about tonight?" Pressed AJ, "She must be psyched to be back in front of a home crowd."

"I guess," said Matty, shrugging his shoulders indifferently while flashing his trademark toothy smile at the camera.

AJ was doing her best to steer Matty away from his shameless self-promotion but before she could ask another question he was hustled off by his security detail.

"I gotta go, Everlasting Love!" He managed to shout, before disappearing through the backstage door while blowing a kiss to the camera, leaving AJ to sign off her interview by saying, "There he goes folks, Matty Brown." As the producer gave her the all clear signal AJ turned to the crew with a 'What the hell was that all about?' gesture.

A couple of blocks away, an ostentatiously large limousine was speeding its way through the Manhattan streets flanked by police outriders, whose blaring sirens warned motorists to clear the way. The frosty atmosphere in the limo's back seat however was in stark contrast to the excitement of the concertgoers at the venue as the star of the show stared sullenly out the window. Beside Kade sat her manager Marvin, who was too engrossed in his telephone to notice that something was amiss. AJ's broadcast was playing on the limo's TV with the sound muted but neither passenger seemed to care.

The silence was eventually broken by Marvin bringing up the tour schedule on his phone and reading it aloud to Kade. "So we've got to be at the airport for 10 am tomorrow morning if we want to get to Baltimore in time for the sound check. After that it's Seattle, LA, San Diego..." he broke off when he realised that Kade wasn't paying attention.

"Are you listening to me?" He snapped. Marvin had been her manager since the very beginning and still spoke to her as if she were that 14 ingénue starting out on the road to fame. He failed to realise that Kade wasn't that little girl anymore, she was an international superstar who took orders from no one and could give as good as she got.

"Yeah, yeah. Airport, sound check, blah blah blah," she replied dismissively.

"What's your problem?" Asked Marvin, irked by her ingratitude for all his hard work and planning.

"My problem?" Said Kade sharply as she turned to face him. "My problem is that everyone in the world knows that I always have white roses in my dressing room."

"So what?" Replied Marvin, failing to see what this had to do with anything.

Before Kade could answer, the limo arrived at the venue, driving past the waiting crowds of reporters before sweeping to a halt outside the backstage door. A large security detail surrounded the car to escort Kade into the arena while keeping the fans and reporters at bay. The long hallway leading to the dressing rooms was lined on both sides by stage crew members, assistants and the ubiquitous hangers-on who always seemed to find their way into the most exclusive of areas and were only ever there to drink free champagne while taking pouty lipped selfies for their Instagram accounts. Kade and her entourage marched resolutely down the corridor ignoring all of that, she was more interested in finishing her argument with Marvin.

"So what?" She continued, picking up exactly where they'd left off in the limo without missing a beat, "I'll tell you so what

Marvin, for the last three nights in a row the roses in my dressing room have been Ivory. Ivory is not white."

"I'm your manager, not a florist," Marvin replied snippily.

"Then manage Marvin, it's not as if I ever ask for much," said Kade, before turning to no-one in particular and shouting "Hydration!" Which prompted a nervous looking intern to rush forward carrying a bottle of high-end mineral water with a straw in the top. Kade took the daintiest of sips before dismissing the assistant with an arrogant wave.

Near the end of the corridor, Matty stood leaning against a wall, openly flirting with two clearly enamoured fans. He quickly broke off however when he spotted Kade approaching.

"There's my special lady," he said, throwing his arms open wide.

"Hey baby," replied Kade as they shared one of those double air kisses that were generally only reserved for business rivals or frenemies. It was a testament to the tenderness of the moment that Kade didn't even bother to break her stride.

"See you after the show?" Called Matty towards the disappearing throng of muscle surrounding Kade.

"I'll dedicate a song to you," she shouted over her shoulder.

"Don't forget to mention my movie, Everlasting Love," he said hopefully but she'd already gone. With nothing else to do, he went back to chatting up his fans.

Kade's entourage stopped at the dressing room door, allowing her to enter alone where she promptly slammed the door on them all leaving everyone outside.

❋ ❋ ❋ ❋ ❋ ❋

As the lights dimmed in the packed auditorium, the atmosphere became charged with anticipation and when the disembodied voice of the announcer proclaimed, "MSG in NYC, give it up for KADE!" The crowd went wild. A burst of light illuminated the stage as the backing musicians and dancers kicked off the opening number of the show while Kade slowly rose from beneath the floor in a swirl of dry ice and lasers. "Hello New York!" She shouted, sending the already excited audience into a frenzy. As the band launched into the first song, Kade made her way to the front of the stage. With the music reaching a crescendo, she raised the microphone to begin singing but nothing came out, causing Kade to throw a confused look towards the wings where Marvin was furiously berating a sound technician.

"Where's the vocal track?" He shouted, trying to be heard over the music.

The technician urgently called the engineer operating the sound desk on his walkie-talkie. "What's going on Tony, where's her vocals?"

"I don't know, we're working on it," the engineer replied, sounding equally as panicked. Marvin grabbed the technician's walkie-talkie and in a rage screamed "Well work faster!"

Out on the stage, Kade was vamping, desperately trying to buy herself time before the crowd could realise that something was amiss.

After what seemed like an eternity, the track containing her vocals finally kicked in over the speakers. The crowd cheered, thinking this was all part of the act, but their support was short lived as the track began to speed up into a high-pitched cartoonish squeal which made it clear to everyone that Kade was in fact miming. The once loyal fans quickly turned into an angry mob, booing and throwing objects at the stage. Having scrimped and saved for months to pay for the overpriced tickets they felt that this was a betrayal of all their years of support.

Kade ran offstage to speak to Marvin, who was still trying to sort out the sound problems in the wings. "What's happening?" She asked anxiously.

"There's something wrong with the tape," said Marvin as he marshalled every crew member he could get his hands on.

"So what am I supposed to do?" Kade continued, becoming increasingly alarmed.

"Go back on and sing," came Marvin's terse reply.

"You know I can't do that," implored Kade.

"Yes you can," snapped Marvin.

"Not anymore!" She said frantically.

"Then you'd better figure something out, and quickly," Marvin told her coldly.

Kade hesitated for a moment, torn between trying to salvage the show or just cutting her losses and running. In the end, the part of her that had been conditioned into believing the show must go on won out, a feeling known only too well by those who'd spent a lifetime performing. It had become second nature to her and so Kade returned to the stage in the vain hope of turning things around.

In spite of her valiant efforts to get the crowd back onside however they were too far gone to care. If Kade hadn't lived in a bubble of five-star hotels, private jets and yachts she would have understood the fans' anger. They had worked their asses off week in week out in retail, nursing and cleaning, saving what little extra money came their way to pay for the exorbitantly priced concert tickets, the travel expenses and the cost of an overnight stay in a New York hotel, just so they could see their idol, and after all that she couldn't even be bothered to sing live for them? If they'd wanted to hear a recording they could have stayed at home and now all that anger and frustration was being directed at Kade. With the audience becoming increasingly hostile, Marvin decided to pull the plug and summoned Kade's security detail.

"Get her off," he ordered.

The four large bodyguards rushed onto the stage and escorted Kade to safety while trying to protect her from the missiles being thrown by the angry fans. The band took that as their cue to stop playing, leaving the show to end in a shambolic mess.

As the venue security tried to deal with the crowd in the auditorium, more trouble was brewing in Kade's dressing room which was now packed with stage crew, security and assistants, with Marvin holding court in the center of the room as the recriminations flew.

"Take your equipment and get the hell out of here," he shouted at the sound team. "You and your crew will never work in this town again!"

"Don't blame us if your act can't sing live," snarled the technician, before throwing his headset on the ground and storming off. The rest of the assistants and crew followed him quickly out the door, not wanting to be next in line for Marvin's ire. With just her manager and bodyguards now left in the room, Kade finally spoke up.

"Tell that sound guy to get back here," she ordered Marvin, "We can fix the tape and go back on."

"It's too late for that," said Marvin defeatedly, "The cat's out of the bag."

"So what happens now?" Demanded Kade, her sense of entitlement beginning to return, "We just sit here and do nothing?"

"I need time to think," said Marvin as he paced the room, "In the meantime we need to get you out of here, it's not safe."

Turning to the security team he barked the order, "Take her back to the hotel."

The bodyguards gathered Kade's belongings and began to usher her towards the door but she hesitated when she realised that Marvin wasn't joining them.

"Aren't you coming?" Asked Kade in a surprised voice.

"No," Marvin replied pensively, "I've got to stay here and try to sort this mess out. You go get a good night's sleep, I'll see you in the morning."

With no time to waste, the security team escorted Kade to the limousine, which made a fast exit from the stage door before they could be spotted. As the convoy pulled away into the New York night, Kade passed angry fans venting their fury as they poured from the venue, She had little sympathy for their plight however and her only thought was, "How dare they."

❋ ❋ ❋ ❋ ❋ ❋

Back in her hotel room, Kade lay on the bed dressed in a white fluffy bathrobe. The champagne and bubble bath she'd enjoyed on returning had helped her get over the initial shock of that evening's proceedings and now that she was back on a more even keel she was looking for answers. Kade picked up the cordless room phone from the bedside table and dialled Marvin's number, which went straight to voicemail without even ringing.

"This is Marvin, leave a message." Went the recording but Kade just hung up annoyed, at least that means he's busy sorting this mess out she reasoned to herself.

Next she tried Matty, but after a couple of rings his phone too went to voicemail.

"This is Matty. I can't come to the phone right now but if you leave a message I'll get back to you. Everlasting Love."

Kade rolled her eyes, did he ever shut up about that movie? "Matty, where are you?" She said angrily after the beep, "I've been trying to get hold of you all night. Call me!"

Boyfriends were supposed to be there for you in your hour of need fumed Kade, how could anyone be so self-centered? As she turned to replace the handset on its base she noticed that the vase on the dresser table contained bright yellow roses. Yellow! Kade threw the handset at the wall before rolling over and pounding her fists on the mattress in a petulant hissy fit.

Chapter 2

As the sun struggled to rise on the bright, crisp New York winter's morning, Kade slept soundly in her room, exhausted from all that had occurred the previous evening. Her dream of sunbathing on a Mediterranean island was rudely interrupted however by the sound of her hotel room door being opened and someone entering unannounced.

Kade jumped up in bed, ripping off her sleep mask to find a stone-faced Marvin using a spare key card to let himself in.

"Hey, you can't just barge in here," she protested, "You could have at least knocked first."

Marvin knocked sardonically on the door before closing it behind him. "Happy now?" He said.

"So did you manage to smooth things over?" Asked Kade.

"See for yourself," replied Marvin as he turned on the TV and began flicking through the morning news channels. Without fail, each of them were showing clips of the fateful concert. Marvin stopped when he got to the channel featuring AJ, the reporter from the live broadcast, who was now in studio and both he and Kade listened intently as she spoke to the news anchor.

"Promoters are said to be cancelling all remaining tour dates as ticket holders across the country demand their money back…" AJ began, but Marvin muted the TV before she could get any further.

"They're cancelling the tour?" Kade exclaimed in disbelief.

"Don't panic," said Marvin stoically, "It's just a knee-jerk reaction. When the fans calm down we'll reschedule."

"Fans?" Snapped Kade, "A bunch of ungrateful losers if you ask me. And where's Matty? I've been calling his phone non-stop but he won't answer."

Marvin just shrugged his shoulders and said, "Can you blame him? He's got a new movie coming out next week, his agent told him he doesn't need the bad publicity."

"Bad publicity? For that pile of garbage?" Kade replied sarcastically. "He plays a vampire's ghost, how can vampires have ghosts Marvin?"

"Listen, I get that you're upset but this is just a temporary blip. I have a PR team working on it as we speak. You just need to lie low for a while until everything blows over."

Marvin was doing his best to placate Kade but she was having none of it.

"So I'm trapped in this hotel room for who knows how long?" Said Kade furiously as she jumped out of bed.

"No, don't be silly. Take a holiday, we'll get you out of the country for a while." Marvin replied, turning on the oily charm that had served him so well in the music business for all those years. As fake as his approach was though, it still made Kade stop and ponder his suggestion.

"I suppose," she eventually conceded. "I hear Aruba is nice this time of year."

"I was thinking of somewhere a bit more secluded," said Marvin, pressing his advantage. "This thing has gone global, meaning the press will have every five-star resort in the world staked out hoping you'll show up."

"So where am I supposed to go?" Kade demanded.

"Leave it to me, there's a private jet on standby at the airport and we've found the perfect place. No one will ever think of looking for you there," Marvin told her, springing closed the trap he'd been luring Kade into all along. Not only would she be out of his hair while he tried to clean this mess up, she'd also think that the whole 'dropping off the radar' thing was her idea.

"Fine, just as long as there's a beach," agreed Kade, before storming into the bathroom to get changed, slamming the door behind her.

❋ ❋ ❋ ❋ ❋ ❋

Kade was in a deep sleep as the private jet made the final approach to its destination. Trying to get from the hotel to the airport without being spotted by the press had been a drag and she was wiped out from all drama.

As the aeroplane began its descent the stewardess gently woke Kade by whispering, "We're coming in to land."

Kade instinctively buckled her seat belt without taking off her sleep mask, which was a pity because she was missing the sight of a spectacular sunset as the plane banked into the clouds. The jet touched lightly down and while it taxied its way along the small runway, Kade finally lifted her mask to look out the window. Noticing that there were no airport buildings or any other signs of habitation she sat suddenly up and shouted to the stewardess in a panic, "Did we just land in a field?"

The stewardess was too busy preparing for disembarkation to take any notice of Kade's query and as the jet came to a halt on the deserted landing strip she went through the post-flight routine of opening the cabin door.

The steps of the plane opened out onto the runway allowing a man in a suit to make his way aboard.

"This is your driver," said the stewardess, introducing the new arrival to Kade.

"Welcome to Ireland," he added cheerfully.

"Ireland?" Replied a confused Kade, still half asleep.

The driver gathered Kade's luggage from the front seats of the plane and headed for the exit.

"If you'd like to follow me?" He said politely.

Still disorientated from having just woken up, Kade dutifully followed him to the door, stopping momentarily at the top of the steps to take in her surroundings while the driver loaded her luggage into the back of a high-end black sedan with tinted windows.

The landscape Kade surveyed may have been green and lush but it was far from tropical.

"You got beaches here?" She called to her driver.

"Hundreds of miles of them," he told her.

"At least that's something," Kade sullenly replied while making her way down the steps. She had barely set foot on the tarmac however when a sudden burst of rain caught her in a heavy downpour, prompting Kade to look skywards and angrily shout, "Seriously?"

They could have been driving for hours or they could have been driving for minutes, it was all the same to Kade, who had instantly fallen asleep as soon as she'd sat into the back of the car. As the driver navigated his way down a small dark road, he found it narrowing to a point where it was barely wide enough to accommodate the car's width. Even though it was a bright moonlit night he was still finding it hard to get his bearings so when they came to a small cottage, barely visible behind a large hedge, he stopped to check the directions he'd been given. The address written on his notepad said 'White Rose Cottage' but the driver couldn't find it anywhere on the map. There seemed no point in checking the car's Sat Nav either as that had gone blank many miles back, save for a spindly threaded line that wound its way across the screen. With no other buildings in sight, and rapidly running out of driveable road, he concluded that this was their destination and so turned to wake Kade.

"We've arrived," said the driver, just loud enough to rouse Kade from her slumber.

Kade lifted her sleep mask and peered bleary-eyed out into the night. "Are you sure?" She asked, sounding unconvinced.

"Positive," lied the driver.

Kade checked her phone but found she had no signal and so, as she tried to shake herself awake, the driver began taking her bags from the car while stacking them neatly by the side of the road. Once he'd retrieved the last of the luggage he opened the rear door, allowing Kade to step gingerly out.

"Where are we?" She asked, trying to get her bearings.

"Killarney," replied the driver.

"You're going to kill me?" Panicked Kade as she took a defensive step backwards.

"No," laughed the driver, "I said Killarney, it's where you're staying," he told Kade as he got back into the car.

"Wait, you're leaving?" Said Kade, confused as to why he was only taking her half of the way.

"I'm only supposed to drop you off."

"Yes, at my luxury hotel."

"That's the address I was given," said the driver, pointing at the rundown cottage.

"This place? It looks like a haunted outhouse," Kade replied scornfully.

"Then it's an ideal place for a Banshee to stay," muttered the driver to himself.

"Pardon me?" Snapped Kade.

"I said it's probably nicer on the inside," he replied with a forced smile.

"And how do you suggest I get in?" Kade demanded.

"The door should be open, they don't get many burglars around here," said the driver starting the engine.

"Or murderers," he added wryly before putting the car into gear and reversing away without waiting for the tip he knew wouldn't be offered.

As the headlights disappeared back up the road, Kade was left standing alone in the moonlight. She had planned to follow the driver on foot and insist he take her back to civilisation but the hoot of an owl soon changed her mind and so, with no other option, she reluctantly began to drag her luggage up the higgledy-piggledy path to the house.

Setting her suitcases down outside the cottage Kade tried the front door, which swung open of its own accord to reveal a pitch black interior.

Kade reached her arm gingerly inside the gloom and, after a moment's fumbling, managed to locate a light switch. It was hardly worth her while turning it on though as the single bulb hanging from the ceiling barely illuminated the cottage's only room, where an old-fashioned brass bed stood in the center. The rest of the cottage seemed to be filled with dusty junk and bric-a-brac which included an ancient pram and rusty bicycle. This was not the secluded getaway she'd been promised and so, in a fit of pique, Kade stamped her foot and screamed "Marvin!!!" at the empty room.

In spite of sleeping her way across the Atlantic, Kade was still exhausted and so began to unpack her night clothes from one of the many suitcases she'd brought with her. As she rummaged around in her luggage for a throw to put over the bed however, a sudden noise from outside startled Kade, forcing her to quickly grab the first thing that came to hand, which she brandished as a weapon towards the invisible peril.

"Who's there?" She called out, waving her curling iron menacingly.

The response was a gentle tapping on the door.

"I warn you, I'm armed," Kade threatened unconvincingly.

Again came the tapping.

Kade looked frantically around the room but there was no escape or hiding place. With the flight option off the table, Kade's fight instinct took over and so, mustering up a temper usually only reserved for paparazzi and incompetent hotel staff, she steeled herself and whipped open the door, surprising the chicken that had been pecking at it from the outside.

The frightened bird fluttered away, squawking and flapping its wings while an equally startled Kade screamed, "Murder! Murder!"

She slammed the door shut and tried unsuccessfully to push an old dresser against it before abandoning her efforts and retreating to the safety of the bed, where she threatened the shadows with her curling iron. Kade tried the phone again but there was still no signal.

"I am so going to fire your ass Marvin!" She yelled at the dead handset before rolling over and screaming angrily into her pillow.

Chapter 3

The soft morning sunlight crept in through the dirty window pane as Kade lay sleeping face down and fully dressed on the bed. The sound of a rooster crowing from somewhere outside half awakened her as she sleepily murmured to herself, "What the hell was that?"

"It's a rooster," replied a voice that definitely wasn't in her imagination.

Kade screamed and jumped up in the bed to be faced by a man in his early thirties, who was standing in the doorway sporting a bemused look on his face.

"Stay back," warned Kade, desperately searching for something to defend herself with.

"Or what?" Smiled the handsome interloper.

"Or this!" Said Kade, instinctively reaching into her suitcase and grabbing a hair dryer which she pointed at the stranger like a gun.

"OK, OK," he said, holding up his hands in mock surrender, "Not the roots."

"I'm serious," said Kade, waving the hair dryer about to make her point.

"Take it easy Goldilocks, I'm not going to harm you," replied the stranger, his tone of voice and mannerisms reminiscent of someone trying to calm a wild horse.

"My name's not Goldilocks!" Snapped a highly offended Kade.

"Then why are you sleeping in my bed?" Asked the stranger.

"You live here?" Said Kade, surveying the mess.

"Nobody lives here," he laughed, "This is my shed."

Now it was Kade's turn to be confused. "I'm supposed to be staying in a shed?" She asked.

The stranger gestured for her to put the hair dryer down and explained, "I think I see what's going on here. My friend rents out a cottage down the road, you must have come to the wrong one. I can take you there if you'd like."

Kade stepped warily off the bed, still not sure whether she should trust this guy.

"How do I know you're not lying to me?" She asked uncertainly.

"You don't," he replied. "You can stay here if you like, I'll only charge you the same rent as you were going to pay in the other place. Fair's fair." He said, turning to leave.

Realising that the obnoxious hayseed was her one shot at getting out of this dump, Kade called him back saying, "Hold on…"

"Sean," said the stranger, stopping in the doorway.

"You can call me Sean."

"Whatever," Kade snarkily replied, "Just give me a chance to get changed."

"No problem," said Sean as he folded his arms and leaned against the doorway.

"Wait outside please?" Demanded Kade.

Sean gave a wry smile and closed the door behind him on his way out.

After what seemed like forever, Kade finally emerged from the cottage dressed to the nines. She was wearing a short white fur coat, skinny jeans and stiletto suede boots with the glamorous ensemble topped off by a pair of those large dark glasses that were designed to provide anonymity while simultaneously drawing attention to the wearer. Kade stopped abruptly at the door however, realising that she was about to step out into a muddy farm yard, with Sean and the farm animals looking on in amusement as her face fell.

"Do you need a hand with your bags?" He offered.

"I can manage," snapped Kade, annoyed that he was finding her predicament so entertaining. Determined to make it across the yard without Sean's help, Kade grabbed her luggage and set forth. She had only taken one step forward however when her heel got stuck in the ground causing her to fall face first into the soft mud, much to the amusement of her newfound nemesis, where she lay for a moment in shock before pulling herself back out of the muck with a sucking sound.

Kade removed her splattered sunglasses to reveal that the only part of her face not covered in mud were two perfectly clean circles around her eyes.

"Need a hand now?" Asked Sean, without leaving his perch on the wall.

Kade screamed a profanity, the nature of which was drowned out by a donkey's braying laugh, while Sean tried to hide his smile as he stepped forward to help her up.

❋ ❋ ❋ ❋ ❋ ❋

It felt to Kade like she'd been walking for miles but in reality they had barely made it 100 meters from the farm. Sean was leading the way carrying the luggage down an uneven dirt track while a muddy Kade stomped peevishly along behind him.

"So where are you from?" Asked Sean in an attempt to lighten the mood.

"Excuse me?" Said Kade, annoyed at having her thoughts of revenge so rudely interrupted.

"I asked where you were from, are you American or Canadian?"

"As if you don't know who I am," replied Kade with a snort of derision.

"And who are you?" Continued Sean, nonplussed.

"Don't play dumb, I know you've seen me on TV," said Kade.

"I don't own a TV."

Kade surveyed the isolated surroundings before muttering, "Why doesn't that surprise me?"

As they rounded the corner, a break in the hedge revealed a picturesque thatched cottage up ahead with a winter blooming flower garden at the front.

"Here we go," said Sean as he led Kade in through the gate and up the path. Taking a key from under the mat, Sean opened the door and brought the suitcases inside. Kade followed him over the threshold and was surprised to find a stylishly decorated interior complete with modern amenities such as a fully fitted kitchen and a pair of comfortable looking armchairs positioned in front of an open fireplace.

"I can give you a guided tour if you like?" Offered Sean once the luggage was safely stored in the hallway.

"I'm fine, just go," said Kade, who'd had enough of his nonsense for one day.

"Whatever you say, your highness," replied Sean, bowing theatrically to make his point.

As he was about to leave, Kade rummaged in her purse for a moment before producing a $100 bill. "Do you have change for a hundred?" She asked, "I haven't got anything smaller."

Sean looked at the note and then back at Kade. "It's fine," he said flatly as he turned to go, "You can catch me some other time."

"Wait," said Kade, suddenly remembering her dilemma, "Do you have a cell phone or a laptop? I need to get in touch with New York."

"I have a carrier pigeon if that's any good to you?" Sean replied, mirroring her own sarcastic manner.

"Forget it." Snapped Kade.

Realising that his reply might have been too rude, Sean's attitude softened. "There's a village not far from here," he relented, "You could try there, just head back the way we came and keep walking, you can't miss it," and with that he left, closing the door behind him.

"Thanks for nothing," Kade shouted at the door, adding "Jerk!" under her breath.

Taking stock of the situation, she looked down at her muddy clothes and sighed deeply. Her New York worries would have to wait for now, or at least until she was looking a tad more presentable.

✳ ✳ ✳ ✳ ✳ ✳

Kade emerged from the en-suite shower wearing a towel, her suitcases open on the bed where she'd laid out a selection of outfits to choose from. Glancing out the window at the rolling hills and then back to her clothes, Kade realised that they were more suited to catwalks and movie premieres rather than the wild Irish countryside. With no other options available however, she wearily tried to cobble together something appropriate to wear.

Despite her best efforts, Kade was still ridiculously overdressed when she left the cottage, wearing a designer jacket, high heel shoes and her ubiquitous dark glasses, grumbling to herself as she struggled to walk the dirt track in her spiked heels. From over a nearby hedge, a sheep was watching the spectacle and bleated as she passed.

"Oh Baa yourself!" Kade retorted, annoyed that even the animals around here were smart alecs.

Kade slogged her way relentlessly down the boreen until she finally came to a crossroads but, with no signposts or road markings to be seen, she quickly became disoriented and found herself lost. Not even able to remember which road she'd just come from, Kade decided to make her way over to a small church that was set back from the side of the road in the hope of finding someone who could give her directions.

Making her way up the windy path at the front, Kade quietly opened the chapel door to find a small group of people rehearsing Christmas carols on the altar. Since they were too engrossed in their singing to notice the newcomer, Kade decided it best not to interrupt and so just stood quietly at the back taking in the atmosphere. It was a rare moment of peace for Kade who'd spent a lifetime surrounded by others and even though the choir had by now finished singing she still didn't have the heart to intrude on such a private moment, instead slipping quietly away, unable to shake the feeling of somehow being a trespasser.

Finding herself back outside and still unsure of which road to take, Kade picked one at random and struck out again, still struggling to walk in her heels. Wobbling her way down the country lane, Kade heard the clopping sound of hooves on stone coming from behind her and, turning to see where the sound was coming from, she found Sean smiling down at her from the seat of a horse and cart.

"Need a lift?" He enquired jovially.

"I'm fine," said Kade abruptly.

"Are you sure," pressed Sean, "It's a long walk."

"I'll manage," replied Kade, determined not to take an ounce of help from this man.

"Please yourself," shrugged Sean, clipping the reins to set his horse off on its way again.

Kade stood aside to let Sean pass but as the cart headed off down the road a sudden thought hit her and so she shouted after him, "Wait! Can you call me an Uber?"

Sean stopped the horse and replied, "Sorry, no Uber."

"No Uber? Can you call me some other car service?"

"No cars."

"No cars? Can you at least call my manager?"

"No phones."

"No phones!" Exclaimed Kade as she stamped her foot in a temper. "I hate this place!"

Sean removed a battered old Gladstone bag from beside him on the seat and gestured for Kade to climb aboard saying, "You're always welcome to hop on?"

"I'd rather walk," she fumed back.

"Don't say I didn't offer," he sighed, gently tapping the reins again which sent the horse off at a leisurely pace while Kade struggled on behind. After only a few steps however, her heel broke causing her to cry out, "You've got to be kidding me," in frustration as she wondered how much more misfortune was to be heaped upon her.

Sean stopped the cart and looked back at Kade holding her broken heel. "Last chance," he said and meant it this time.

Realising that she was out of options, Kade reluctantly accepted the offer of a ride. There was no way she was sitting up front though, that seat looked far too small to fit them both without some form of physical contact and so Kade decided to take her customary place in the rear.

Clambering onto the tail of the cart she sat perched on the edge with her back to Sean but, as the cart lurched forward, Kade was forced into an undignified scramble in order to keep herself upright.

"You need to be more careful," laughed Sean, unable to hide his amusement.

"If I want your advice I'll ask for it," said Kade sourly as her face flushed with embarrassment. The only thing she was grateful for was that there were no photographers around to capture her indignity for posterity.

"I wasn't telling *you* to be careful," replied Sean, "I was talking to Sally."

"Who's Sally?" Asked Kade, annoyed by this cryptic line of conversation.

"This is Sally," said Sean, leaning forward and giving his horse a gentle pat on her hind quarters, making Sally whinny and buck slightly.

"You're in a cantankerous mood today," Sean remarked.

"That's no way to speak to your horse," said Kade disapprovingly.

"I was talking to you," said Sean over his shoulder, which only reignited Kade's temper.

"You know what," she replied indignantly, "Why don't you just stick to the driving and save the chit chat for the animals Doctor Doolittle."

"If you say so," shrugged Sean.

"I do."

"Your choice."

"Yes it is!" Said Kade emphatically, folding her arms and huffing at the impertinence of this guy.

Just as she thought she'd gotten the last word however, Kade's self-righteous indignation was shattered when the cart hit a pothole splashing mud up onto her clean clothes. It took all of Sean's willpower to hold in his laughter while Kade, too shocked and angry to speak, just stared at her ruined clothes in furious disbelief.

❄ ❄ ❄ ❄ ❄ ❄

The local village, like so many others dotted around the countryside, consisted of one small street made up of those few businesses essential to an isolated community, namely a garage, a general store/post office, a funeral directors and a pub. The place was unusually busy that afternoon as most of the shopkeepers were out on the street putting Christmas decorations up on their storefronts and even the undertaker was joining in, although his adornments were on the more tasteful and muted side.

As the cart made its way up the street, everyone stopped to take in the sight of the bedraggled stranger sitting on the back, who seemed like she was going to explode in a fiery ball of rage at any moment.

Having reached the middle of the village, Sean brought his horse to a sudden halt, which sent Kade rolling onto her back.

"We've arrived," he announced.

Kade struggled to get back into an upright position while simultaneously trying to hide her embarrassment from the locals, who'd all stopped what they were doing to watch.

"Arrived where?" Demanded Kade as she took in her surroundings. "You said you'd take me to town."

"And here we are your majesty," replied Sean with an exaggerated flourish of his hand.

"This is not a town," stated Kade, "Where are all the nail salons? The boutiques? The coffee shops?"

"Bridget over there has everything you need," said Sean, pointing to the small general store.

"In that little place? I doubt it," Kade replied sceptically as she sized up the quaint storefront.

"Well I'm afraid it's the best you're going to get, do you need help getting down?" Asked Sean, holding out his hand.

"I'll manage," snapped Kade, rebuffing his offer and instead rolling over onto her front to wiggle clumsily backwards off the cart.

"I'll be passing by this way later if you need a ride back?" Sean offered.

"I won't be going back," Kade replied as she finally made it down off the cart, "As soon as I get hold of my manager I'm out of here."

"If you say so," said Sean with a dubious smile.

"I do say so."

"See you later then."

"No you won't!"

Sean clipped the reins and the cart headed off again on its travels, leaving Kade stranded in the middle of the street. The onlookers were still staring in curious amusement until a shout of "And what are you looking at?" from the mercurial new arrival sent them scurrying back about their business while Kade angrily stomped her way over to the general store.

As she entered the shop, Kade was hit by a comforting blast of warm air coming from a large open fire. The shopkeeper, a homely woman in a flowery dress and apron, was standing on a stool putting up Christmas decorations but paused when she heard the bell above the shop door ring. She turned to find Kade limping up to the counter holding her broken shoe in one hand.

"Mother of God, are you alright love?" Said the worried shopkeeper, scrambling down off the stool when she saw the state of Kade.

"Do I look alright?" Came Kade's exhausted reply.

Pulling up a stool, the shopkeeper offered it to Kade saying, "Here, sit down before you fall down, can I get you something to drink?"

Kade flopped wearily down and considered the shopkeeper's offer for a moment. "Maybe a Mimosa?" She mused, "What Champagnes do you have?"

"I'm sorry, I don't have any Champagne. I have tea?" Suggested the shopkeeper.

"Mint, Cranberry, Cinnamon? What flavour?"

"Tea flavour," said the shopkeeper bluntly.

"Fine, whatever," Kade acquiesced with a sigh.

"I'm Bridget by the way," said the shopkeeper as she went into the small kitchen situated behind the counter. "Would I be right in saying you're not from around here?" She continued through the open door.

"I don't even know where here is," admitted Kade.

Bridget brought out two steaming hot mugs of tea and handed one to Kade. "You really are lost, aren't you?" She said sympathetically.

Kade's brash front slipped and for the first time she seemed truly defeated. "You don't know the half of it," she replied downheartedly.

Sensing the mood, Bridget reached behind the counter and produced a small bottle of whiskey saying, "Here, let me cheer up that tea for you," as she poured a generous shot into Kade's cup.

"I thought you didn't have any drink?"

"I said I didn't have any Champagne. Champagne's not a real drink, it's just fizzy wine," smiled Bridget, while pouring an equally generous measure into her own mug.

As Bridget put the bottle back behind the counter, the shop door opened with a tinkle and a local man in his late fifties entered. He'd barely gotten half way across the doorstep however when Bridget shouted, "Get out Martin!" Causing the shocked customer to quickly shuffle back outside, closing the door behind him. "This is no time for men," laughed Bridget, bringing a much needed smile to Kade's face.

"Cheers," said Kade, holding up her tea.

"Sláinte," replied Bridget as they clinked mugs and took two large, badly needed mouthfuls of Bridget's special brew.

"So what is it you do?" Asked Bridget as she settled back in her chair for a good natter.

"Do?" Replied a confused Kade.

"Yes, do," continued Bridget, as if it was the most obvious question in the world.

"You don't know me?" Said Kade, not sure if Bridget was being serious.

"Should I?" Asked Bridget genuinely.

"No, I guess you shouldn't," smiled Kade, pleasantly surprised that for the first time in her life she was happy not to be recognised.

"Are you over here on holidays?" Continued Bridget, pumping the new arrival for gossip.

"You could call it that," replied Kade, not even sure herself what she was doing there.

"Good for you, everyone deserves a break," said Bridget cheerily as she took another hearty swig of her tea.

Kade considered Bridget's statement for a moment before replying, "You're right, I do deserve it, I can't remember the last time I had a break."

"So are you living locally?" Bridget queried. She was asking more questions than a reporter but was doing it in such a gentle and disarming manner that Kade found herself unwittingly opening up.

"I'm staying in a, I guess you'd call it a cottage? I'm not really sure where it is though, or how I'm even going to get back there," said Kade, suddenly realising how much her regimented life had changed in the past 48 hours.

"Well that shouldn't be too difficult to figure out," advised Bridget as she put a comforting hand on Kade's arm.

"It won't?" Asked Kade, curious to find out what kind of investigative powers this seemingly innocuous shopkeeper possessed.

"Well since there's only one cottage for rent in the area and the owner is a friend of mine I think we can narrow down our options."

"Really?" Replied Kade, perking up slightly at the fact that something was finally going her way.

"Yes, I'll call her now," said Bridget, producing a cell phone from her apron pocket, much to Kade's surprise.

"You have phones here?" She asked Bridget in disbelief.

"Of course we have," replied Bridget with a quizzical look. "Do you not have phones where you come from?"

"We do but..." Kade was about to explain her argument with Sean but was cut short as Bridget put the phone to her ear. Gesturing for Kade to hold her thought, Bridget said, "One minute now and I'll get someone to drive you back."

Now Kade was both surprised and annoyed. "You have phones *and* cars?"

This tickled Bridget to no end. "We're Irish, not Amish," she laughed before going out the back of the shop to make her call.

"Wait until I get my hands on him," muttered Kade as she downed the rest of her whiskey laced tea.

Bridget and Kade were on their third mug when a late-model family SUV pulled up on the street outside. A young woman got out and entered the shop to find Bridget laughing heartily as a clearly annoyed Kade recounted the story of how she'd met Sean that morning.

"And he told you there were no cars or telephones?" Said Bridget as the tears rolled down her face.

"You're starting early Bridget," commented the new arrival as she spotted the bottle of spirits on the floor between them both.

"Oh hush," chided Bridget, "It's medicinal."

"I'll be the judge of that," the young woman replied with a disapproving smile.

"This is Emer," said Bridget making the introductions, "She's the local doctor."

Emer offered her hand to greet Kade saying, "Pleased to meet you...?"

Kade paused for a beat before replying, "Kate, I'm Kate," as she shook Emer's hand.

"She's your new house guest," added Bridget, filling in the gaps that Kade had left out.

"So I've been told," said Emer, "I'm sorry I wasn't there to meet you on arrival but I was called away to an emergency on the Murphy farm."

"Nothing serious I hope?" Asked Bridget with a slightly worried tone, as small villages in Ireland were more like big families.

"It was for Mr Murphy," laughed Emer, "His wife's just given birth to twins."

"Well I'll drink to that!" Cheered Bridget as she reached for the whisky bottle.

"Bridget?" Said Emer sternly.

"What? It's just a small one, to wet the babies' heads," Bridget protested, while offering a top up to Kade who politely demurred.

"Is there anyone else staying with you Kate?" Asked Emer, changing the subject so as to avoid giving Bridget a public health lecture in front of their guest. "It's just that it was a last minute online booking and they didn't give me much information."

"No, it's just me," replied Kade. "But I don't think I'll be sticking around," she added hurriedly, suddenly remembering what had brought her there in the first place.

"Well you're welcome to stay as long as you like," said Emer warmly, "I'm heading back to the cottage now if you'd like a lift?"

"That would be great," Kade gratefully replied as she got up to leave. "Thank you so much for the tea," she said, bidding farewell to Bridget. "You don't know how much I needed it."

"No problem, be sure to call again if you ever need a *chat,*" winked Bridget while discreetly waving the whisky bottle so that Emer wouldn't see.

"Thanks, I will," said Kade as she made her way to the door, leaving Bridget to pour herself another tot.

"And I think you've had enough for one day Bridget," Emer reprimanded in her best Doctor's voice. "You're only supposed to wet the babies' heads, not give them a full shampoo and rinse."

"Yes mammy," replied Bridget as she contritely put the bottle down to wave Emer and Kade off. As soon as the door closed behind them however, Bridget poured herself another shot with an impish grin. The bell chimed as Martin came back to try and do his shopping for a second time only to be greeted with another "Get out Martin!" From Bridget, which sent him shuffling back out the door once more, grousing to himself.

❋ ❋ ❋ ❋ ❋ ❋

"You'll have to excuse Bridget," apologised Emer as she drove Kade back home down the country roads. "She's not normally so... festive."

"It's fine, I liked her. She was kind of cool," replied Kade, who had been admiring the scenery from the car window, more able to appreciate its beauty in the daylight and when she wasn't struggling to walk in a broken heel.

"Cool?" Laughed Emer. "Are you sure that's not the whiskey talking?"

"Maybe just a little," said Kade, allowing herself a chuckle.

As the laughter subsided, Kade seemed to slip back into a world of her own.

"You don't seem to be dressed for the countryside," Emer remarked, stealing a sideways glance at Kade's outfit.

"I had to pack in a hurry," replied Kade, in a tone that made it clear she didn't feel like elaborating.

"We can stop at my place," said Emer, not pushing any further, "I'll lend you something more suitable to wear."

"I don't want to put you out."

"You're a guest, it's no bother."

Kade was about to reply when the car passed Sean coming in the opposite direction on his horse and cart. Emer gave him a friendly beep of the horn and Sean returned the greeting, making a special point of waving to Kade who threw him a dirty look in return.

"Do you know that guy?" She asked Emer once they'd passed.

"Who, Sean?" Emer replied, "We've been friends since we were kids, we did everything together, school, communion, confirmation. We even went to the same college."

"He's a doctor too?" Said Kade dubiously.

"No, he's a vet, which he claims is harder than being a doctor because animals can't tell you where it hurts."

"Sounds like something that jackass would say," huffed Kade.

Emer shot her a look of curiosity but didn't pursue the comment any further. They drove the rest of the short journey in silence until they reached their destination, a modern dormer bungalow set amid a generous lawn.

"Here we are," said Emer, pulling into the driveway and parking outside the house. "Home, sweet home."

As Emer got out of the car, Kade undid her seat belt and waited for the passenger door to be opened as was customary in her world. When Emer just breezed past and went into the house, the realisation hit Kade that around here she wasn't the center of attention and so, forced to let herself out of the car, Kade quickly followed Emer to the front door before her embarrassment became apparent.

"Hello?" Called Kade as she stepped tentatively into the hallway.

"I'm just digging out some clothes for you," Emer shouted from one of the bedrooms. "Head into the kitchen and stick the kettle on, make yourself at home."

"OK?" Replied Kade uncertainly.

Emer's house was barely a tenth the size of the one Kade lived in but it still took her three attempts to find the right door. When she did finally manage to locate the kitchen, Kade took the electric kettle from the countertop and turned it over in her hands as she tried to figure out how it worked. She had just managed to find the button that popped the lid open when she was interrupted by two kids coming rushing in through the back door.

"Oh!" Exclaimed Kade, getting such a start that she almost dropped the kettle.

Truth be told she hadn't much experience dealing with children, if these even were children? Maybe it was the fact that they were both wearing Santa hats which added to the confusion. Were they elves? Or even Leprechauns? This was Ireland after all, it was at times like this that Kade wished she'd paid more attention when people told her things.

"Hello," said the little girl, who seemed mature beyond her nine years.

"Are you supposed to be here?" Enquired a clearly flustered Kade.

"Yes," replied the little girl politely, "Are you?"

"I'm waiting for the Doctor," Kade awkwardly answered.

Although Kade had many fans around this girl's age, she had only ever met them at the highly stage managed meet and greets she was sometimes forced to do. Apart from that, Kade never encountered kids in the wild as none of her friends had children, and by friends she meant Marvin and whatever guy she was dating at that particular moment.

"Don't worry," said the little girl as she took in Kade's dishevelled appearance, "Our mam is the best Doctor in the world, she'll make you better."

"Thank you?" Kade replied, unsure of how to take the remark.

The girl gently liberated the kettle from Kade's hands and filled it under the tap before turning it on. The little boy meanwhile was staring silently at Kade as only eight year old kids have a knack of doing. It was making her feel uncomfortable and for a moment she considered giving him some money to make him stop. The boy eventually broke eye contact to take a pen and paper from his school bag. "Can you sign this for me?" he asked, proffering them to Kade.

"Oh, I don't really do autographs," she said, slightly embarrassed.

The little boy seemed puzzled by this remark. "I don't want your autograph," he replied, "I want your signature. It's a petition to save the barn owl."

"Oh, sorry, OK," said Kade, turning to sign the petition on the counter so as to hide her blushes. She could still hear the children whispering loudly behind her even though they thought they were being discreet.

"Why did she think I wanted her autograph?" The little boy asked his sister.

"She's American," explained the girl, "They all think they're famous."

Thankfully Kade was saved from further embarrassment by Emer coming into the kitchen carrying an armful of jeans and sweaters. "I hope you two aren't annoying our guest?" She said to the children.

"No mum, she's just autographing my petition," replied the little boy, as an elbow in the ribs from his sister sent them both into a fit of giggles.

"These are my kids, Molly and Patrick," said Emer, introducing them to Kade.

"We've met," replied Kade, so awkwardly that it set the kids off laughing again.

"Alright giggly Magees," interrupted Emer, "Homework time."

"But mum, we need to unwind first," protested Patrick.

"So unwind with your schoolbooks, and don't take all night, your Dad is video calling at six."

Molly and Patrick reluctantly took their school bags and headed to their rooms to begin the homework assignments while Emer put the pile of clothes on the kitchen table. "These should fit you, we're about the same size," she told Kade.

While Emer set about making the tea Kade began sorting through the clothes. To make conversation Kade asked, "Are you and their father not together?" Not realising that in some situations this may have been seen as intrusive. That was Kade's problem, she had no one in her life to correct her when she spoke out of turn which is why she often came across as brash and insensitive even when she hadn't meant to.

If Emer had been offended though she didn't show it and replied, "We are normally but my husband Liam is away on business at the moment. He's been gone for the past month but he'll be home for Christmas."

"That'll be nice," replied Kade as she pulled a comfortable looking Aran sweater from the pile of clothes.

Emer handed Kade a cup of tea telling her, "I'm afraid I don't have anything stronger than this."

"That's fine," smiled Kade gratefully, "I think I've had enough whiskey for one day anyway."

"There's a utility room to the left," said Emer, noticing the sweater in Kade's hand. "You can try it on in there if you like."

Kade went to change in the little room off the kitchen but left the door ajar so she could still speak to Emer.

"I thought maybe you and the vet had a thing?" Asked Kade, her innate nosiness getting the better of her.

"What, me and Sean? Yuck, it'd be like kissing me baby brother."

Kade smiled to herself at the way Emer pronounced *'me baby brudder'*. There was a lilt to her voice and genuine warmth in the way she spoke which was something Kade didn't encounter very often in her line of work.

"It's just that you said you were close." Kade continued.

"We are, but not in that way," Emer explained. "He's more like my wingman."

"Wingman?" Said Kade, sticking her head back around the door in surprise.

Emer laughed at the astonished look on Kade's face. "It's a joke we have between us, Sean introduced me to my husband Liam."

"Is he from around here too?"

"No, Liam and I met in college, he was Sean's roommate. I was in my first year of medicine, Sean was doing his vet thing and Liam was studying to be an engineer, a right little gang of tearaways we were."

"So you all lived in the city?"

"Yes, our wild student days, although by the end I was the only student left. Liam qualified first and went off to build bridges, then Sean got his degree and landed a fancy position working for the government."

"If he was getting on so well in the city then what's he doing back here?" Asked Kade, who for someone that claimed to detest Sean, was asking an awful lot of questions about him.

"His parents were getting too old to manage the farm and since Sean was an only child he came home to help them run the place," Emer continued. "Sadly they both passed away last year, his mother died in May and his dad went a couple of weeks later. They said it was a broken heart."

"I'm sorry, I didn't mean to pry," replied Kade contritely.

Emer smiled and gave her guest a reassuring pat on the arm. "You're not prying, you're just getting to know your neighbours."

Although Emer's manner was disarming, Kade knew that she shouldn't press any further but something inside her really wanted to hear the end of the story which is why she eventually asked, "So why didn't he go back to his job?"

"He thought about it but he doesn't have the heart to sell the farm," Emer sighed, "And he says that the people around here need him more."

"What about you, don't you miss living in the city?"

"Sometimes," said Emer wistfully. "It's a funny thing though, no matter how often you leave or where you go in the world, Killarney always calls you home."

They both instinctively gazed out the window at the green fields, lit golden by the setting sun, and for a moment Kade could believe it was true.

Their reverie was interrupted by Patrick and Molly coming back into the kitchen to announce, "Homework's finished!"

"Right, get washed up for dinner so," said Emer, snapping back into mammy mode. "Would you like to stay and have something to eat Kate?"

"I'm fine, thanks. I have to get back."

"Do you need a lift?"

"Is it far?"

Emer opened the back door and pointed to a cottage which sat not a hundred yards down the lane. "Far enough for you?" she smiled.

"I think I can make it," laughed Kade.

"Well I've stocked the place with plenty of food and supplies but if you need anything just let me know."

"There is one thing, do you know where I can make a telephone call?" Asked Kade. "I can't get a signal on my cell phone."

"Let me see?" Said Emer, taking Kade's phone and tapping the screen a few times before handing it back. "The signal is fine, you just needed to sign in to the network. I've popped my number into your contacts too, just in case of emergencies."

"Thank you so much, and for the clothes. I don't have any local currency on me at the moment but…"

"You don't have to give me money, they're free."

"Oh, I didn't mean to offend you," added Kade hurriedly.

Emer just laughed, "I'm actually flattered that someone would consider paying me for my castoffs."

"This is really generous of you," said Kade, relieved that she hadn't made yet another faux pas. "Thanks again for everything."

"You're welcome, don't be a stranger," said Emer, letting Kade out through the back door and watching as she made her way down to the end of the garden and through the gap in the hedge to the road.

Kade had barely gone ten steps from Emer's gate however when she was startled by a voice from behind her announcing, "Well look who it is."

Kade turned to see Sean coming up the road behind her, leading his donkey home from the nativity rehearsals at the church.

"Can I not get one minute away from you?" Fumed Kade as the frustration rose up inside her like a volcano about to erupt. What was it about this guy that could provoke such a visceral reaction in her at a mere moment's notice?

"I nearly didn't recognise the princess without her fancy clothes," Sean remarked to his donkey.

That was it, Kade wasn't going to let some hick speak to her as if she was a nobody and so she shouted, "Listen buster, I've had just about enough of you and your smart mouth. Do you know who I am?"

"You keep asking me that. Do you genuinely not know who you are?" Sean smiled in that infuriating manner of his, "Amnesia is a serious condition, you should really see a Doctor," he continued.

Sean's smugness lasted all of five seconds as it now became his turn to be startled by a voice from behind.

"She is seeing a Doctor," came Emer's voice, "Me!"

Sean's face dropped when he realised that Emer had overheard their whole conversation and all he could muster was an embarrassed, "Oh."

"Oh, is right!" Scolded Emer as she stared him down with folded arms and a face like thunder.

"I'm in trouble aren't I?" Said Sean, like a small boy who had just been caught stealing apples from an orchard.

"Yes you are," continued Emer, "Inside, now!" she ordered, pointing at her house.

"But what about my donkey?" Pleaded Sean.

"Oh I have plenty of room for a donkey," said Emer, "And an ass!" She added pointedly.

Suitably chastened, Sean bowed his head like a naughty schoolboy and led the donkey through the gap in the hedge while Emer gave Kade a secret smile and a wink before following him up the path.

❋ ❋ ❋ ❋ ❋

Back in her own cottage, Kade put the bags of clothes on the kitchen table and opened her phone. Although her inbox was showing no new emails she still checked her voicemail in the hopes that someone, anyone, had tried to get in touch.

Kade just sighed when the automated voice said, "You have no new messages," too exhausted to even throw a tantrum anymore. Instead she put the phone away and attempted to make herself dinner.

Even a child can feed themselves at a push but for someone like Kade, who'd spent their whole life being waited on hand and foot, cooking a simple meal was anything but.

First Kade tried to open a tin of soup, using a corkscrew she'd found in the knife drawer, which went about as well as you'd expect. After draining the contents into a pot through the small, corkscrew shaped hole in the top of the can, Kade tried to heat the pot on the stove but couldn't figure out how to turn it on. This had looked a whole lot easier when her private chef was doing all the work. Abandoning the soup, Kade instead tried to microwave a whole chicken that she'd found in the fridge but when that wouldn't fit inside the small compartment she instead tried to heat up some steaks from the freezer. Kade stuffed the foil tray in the microwave and jabbed the buttons randomly until it came to life.

"Finally," she thought to herself, "This cooking business isn't so hard after all, maybe I should open my own restaurant someday."

Kade's dreams of culinary greatness went quickly out the window however when the foil inside the microwave began to fizzle and spark, causing her to run screaming out of the room in a panic. When the timer finally pinged to a halt, she peered cautiously around the door as smoke billowed about the kitchen.

Twenty minutes later, Kade was lying in bed eating cereal straight from the box. To take her mind off the disaster in the kitchen, she redialled Marvin's phone number which went directly to voicemail as before.

"This is Marvin, leave a message."

Oh she was going to leave a message alright.

"It's me Marvin, *again*! Don't keep ignoring my calls, I'm still your boss."

Kade furiously jabbed the button to end the call and without missing a beat hit Matty's number in the speed dial. This too went straight to the now familiar voicemail.

"I can't come to the phone right now but if you leave a message I'll get right back to you. Everlasting love."

"Still with the dumb greeting," Kade seethed, such a narcissist, what did she ever see that guy? Besides his rock-hard abs, and his cute smile and...

Kade quickly hung up without leaving a message, not wanting to be lulled into saying something she'd regret by the thoughts of Matty's movie star good looks. She surveyed her humble surroundings for a moment before putting her phone on the nightstand and rolling over to go to sleep with a sigh of resignation.

Chapter 4

The morning sun was barely up as Martin made his way towards the pasture to milk the cows. As he passed by White Rose Cottage a rooster crowed in the yard and from somewhere inside the house a woman's voice could be heard shouting, "Shut the hell up!"

It was a good three hours later when Kade finally made her way down to the kitchen, wearing the comfortable pyjamas and dressing gown that Emer had given her. While going through the presses looking for something to make breakfast with, Kade found a jar of instant coffee. She tried to follow the instructions on the label but quickly became frustrated and so took out her phone instead.

"Siri, how do you make instant coffee?" She asked.

"First you boil some water," came the reply.

Kade gave the range of appliances on the counter a cursory glance before asking,

"Siri, how do you work an electric kettle?"

At a farm about five fields over, Sean was in a barn, carefully examining a heavily pregnant cow as the farmer watched anxiously from the doorway.

"It looks like she's ready to give birth," said Sean.

"How long before she goes do you reckon?" Asked the farmer.

"Probably sometime in the next twenty-four hours," advised Sean.

"Do you think she'll be alright?" Said the worried farmer, "We nearly lost her the last time."

"She should be fine, but if there are any complications call me straight away."

"I'll do that, thanks again," replied the farmer gratefully.

Sean returned to his car and was pulling out of the farm onto the narrow lane when he came across Emer driving in the opposite direction. As was customary in these parts, they both stopped and rolled down their windows to talk.

"You on a house call too?" She enquired.

"Calving," replied Sean, "What's yours?"

"Colic."

"Rather you than me."

"Likewise," laughed Emer.

"I'll talk to you later?"

"Sure, and don't forget what I told you," she said in an admonishing tone that was only semi-humorous.

"Yes mammy," smiled Sean to himself as Emer drove off.

The once clean counter top in the White Rose Cottage kitchen was now covered with torn bags of flour, sugar, spilled coffee grounds, opened cartons of milk and other detritus. Meanwhile, Kade sat at the kitchen table, happily drinking a single cup of coffee which tasted all the better for having made it herself, (with the assistance of numerous YouTube videos, naturally.) Her self-congratulatory mood was interrupted by her phone suddenly ringing and she nearly sent the coffee mug flying as she scrambled to answer it.

"Hello? Marvin? Matty?" Answered Kade, desperate to hear a familiar voice.

"Only me I'm afraid," replied Emer from the other end of the line.

"Oh," said Kade, slumping back onto her chair.

Emer could hear the disappointment in Kade's voice prompting her to ask, "Did I call at a bad time?"

"No, it's fine," Kade replied as she tried to regain her composure. "What's up?"

"I was just ringing to find out how you were settling in."

"Alright, I guess," lied Kade.

"And I was wondering if you fancied coming over for dinner tonight? I don't like the thought of you eating alone."

"Thanks for the offer but I think I'll pass," replied Kade, who was in no mood to be sociable.

"Are you sure?"

As Kade looked around at the messy kitchen, the sight of the failed attempts at making the previous night's meal prompted a sudden change of heart. "You know what," she told Emer, "On second thoughts I will come, thanks."

"That's settled so, how does six sound?" Suggested Emer.

"Perfect, see you then."

"The weather today is supposed to be lovely by the way," added Emer, dropping a not so subtle hint. "You should go for a walk and take in the sights."

"I'm kind of busy at the moment, but thanks for the suggestion," said Kade, who'd walked down more than enough country roads to last her a lifetime.

"No buts. Fresh air, Doctor's orders," Emer insisted, sounding as if she wasn't going to take no for an answer.

"If you say so," replied Kade, resisting the urge to add 'Mom' to the end of the sentence.

Having ended the call, Kade drained her cup and took it to the sink. She looked at the messy countertop and then at her phone which was still showing no messages.
With nothing else in the house to occupy her, Kade resigned herself to her fate, grabbed a coat from the rack and headed for the door.

Emer wasn't lying about the weather, although the sky was cloudy a small gap had opened up to reveal a beautiful patch of blue allowing a surprisingly warm ray of December sun to shine on Kade's face. Not as warm as Aruba mind you, a fact which wasn't lost on her.

Making her way down the lane, a far easier task now that she was dressed more appropriately for the countryside, Kade began to recognise landmarks from her previous days' travels. She passed the shed where she'd mistakenly spent her first night, and slept surprisingly well given the circumstances. She also passed the farmyard where she'd unceremoniously landed face first in the mucky muck, a memory which still rankled. At least that Sean guy was nowhere to be seen this time, the last thing she needed was him further antagonising her.

As Kade approached the crossroads it began to lightly rain so she ran towards the church for shelter, having learned that around here, heavier downpours were never far behind.

Kade slowly pushed open the church door and peered inside to see if the coast was clear. Finding the place deserted she entered and began to explore, admiring the Christmas decorations as they glistened in the candlelight. The oldfashioned organ at the top of the church reminded Kade of one her grandmother used to own and when she sat on the stool to have a closer look, Kade's hands instinctively rested on the keys and began to play.

The sound of the Christmas carol, a favourite of hers from childhood, echoed around the church while she lost herself in the music. As the piece finished however, Kade was snapped back to reality by gentle applause coming from behind the altar.

"Chopin if I'm not mistaken," said the white haired priest who appeared from the sacristy, "Very fitting under the circumstances."

Kade had believed she was alone and so her only reply was a flustered, "I'm sorry, I didn't mean to be disrespectful."

"There's no need to apologise," said the priest warmly, "It sounded wonderful, even if it is a bit different from the kind of music you normally play."

"You know who I am?" Said Kade, startled that, of all the people she'd encountered in the last few days, this elderly priest was the only one to recognise her.

"There's no need to sound so surprised," he chuckled, "I'm a priest, not a hermit."

Kade blushed at the thought of embarrassing herself yet again but was put at ease by the priest adding, "Although I'm more of a country and western fan myself."

"I just wanted to see what the organ sounded like, I hope I didn't disturb you?" Said Kade remorsefully.

"Not at all," replied the priest, "You should hear how our regular organist plays, now that's disturbing."
This prompted an involuntary laugh from Kade.

"It's nice to have someone who knows what they're doing for a change," he continued, "You obviously enjoy it, do you play much?"

"Not as often as I'd like to," she replied.

Finding herself suddenly overcome with a rush of painful memories, Kade stood up to leave with a hurried, "I should go."

"Well the door is always open," said the priest, sensing her sadness, "My name is Father John, and you're welcome here anytime."

"I'm not really religious," Kade awkwardly admitted.

"Me neither," Father John whispered conspiratorially, "I only do this job so I can dress like Johnny Cash," which made Kade laugh again in spite of her melancholy.

"Thanks again for letting me play," she told him as she hurriedly headed for the door.

Once Kade had gone, Father John quietly closed the organ lid and smiled to himself.

Chapter 5

Emer was busy cooking in the kitchen when a knock came to the back door. "Can somebody get that for me please?" She shouted into the dining room as Patrick dutifully came running into the kitchen to answer the door.

"I hope I'm not too early?" Said Kade as she entered.

"You're just in time, make yourself at home," replied Emer, who was busy checking the oven.

"Whoa!" Kade exclaimed when she realised that the kitchen had undergone a dramatic change since her last visit.

What had previously been a modern but utilitarian affair was now transformed into a scene out of a Hallmark Christmas movie. From the oak beams that supported the ceiling hung green and red garlands of holly and ivy, and not the plastic kind either, actual real holly and ivy that had been picked directly off the bush at the end of the garden. There wasn't a spare surface in the room that hadn't been festooned with red and gold decorations with the scene being completed by an open log fire and a TV in the corner of the room where Bing Crosby and David Bowie were singing 'Little Drummer Boy'.

"This looks amazing," said an awestruck Kade.

"It looks like something Santa sneezed into a hanky," Emer admitted jokingly, "But the kids wanted to do something special for when their dad gets home."

"I'm sorry I didn't bring anything," said Kade, suddenly conscious of the fact that she'd shown up empty handed. "I went to buy you something in the village but when I reached the crossroads I got lost and somehow kept going around in circles."

"That does tend to happen a lot around here," said Emer with a smile.

"Is there anything I can do to help?" Kade asked, secretly hoping that Emer wouldn't say yes and force her to reveal a complete lack of culinary skills.

"No, everything's under control," Emer replied, just as one of the pots boiled over. "Well, almost under control."

Kade grabbed a tea towel to help Emer but was stopped in her tracks by the sight of Sean coming into the kitchen from the dining room carrying a handful of cutlery.

"I've set the table but we're short on spoons," he began but faltered when he saw Kade. "Oh, it's you," he said, genuinely surprised.

"What's he doing here?" Kade furiously demanded.

"I could ask you the same question," said Sean, who seemed equally as unhappy to see Kade.

"I'm not staying if he is," Kade pouted.

"Well I don't see anybody rushing to stop you leaving," Sean retorted.

They were about to launch into round three of their on-going argument but the shindy was interrupted by Emer spinning suddenly around and menacing them both with her wooden spoon.

"Now listen here the pair of you," she declared, "I'm sick of this childish carry on. You're both going to kiss and make up, understand me?"

Kade and Sean were both horrified by Emer's ultimatum.

"What?" Shrieked Kade.

"You can't be serious," pleaded Sean.

Emer had to stifle a laugh when it dawned on her what she'd just said. "Alright, maybe that was a bad choice of words," she conceded, "You don't have to kiss but you do have to make up."

"I should go, I have a farm to tend to," said Sean, grabbing his coat.

"And I have a kitchen to clean," added Kade.

They were both about to go their separate ways when Emer's commanding voice stopped them in their tracks. "Freeze!" She ordered, "I've spent all day getting this dinner ready so nobody is going anywhere."

"But…"

"No buts Mister! There's more spoons in the drawer, get that table set and then help the kids with the decorations."

"Fine," said Sean, sullenly grabbing spoons from the drawer.

Kade smirked at Sean as he made his way back into the dining room but was quickly pulled up by Emer, who told her, "And you Missy, open that bottle of wine and don't stop pouring until I tell you!"

Kade quickly obeyed, not wanting to draw Emer's wrath as the wooden spoon looked lethal in her hands.

❋ ❋ ❋ ❋ ❋ ❋

As Emer, Molly and Patrick happily tucked into their dinners, Kade and Sean ate in stony silence, pausing only to throw the occasional glare at each other. There wasn't enough wine in the world to thaw those two out but, ever the optimist, Emer tried to lighten the mood by saying, "Well this is nice," which made Molly and Patrick giggle at the patent untruth.

Emer ignored their sniggers and continued, "Sean, don't you have something to say to Kate?"

"No, I don't think so."

"Something we discussed earlier?" Emer prompted.

"Nope."

"Are you sure?" Said Emer, this time adding an ominous emphasis to her words.

"Positive," said Sean, refusing to make eye contact.

Emer sighed as she put her knife and fork down saying, "I was hoping it wouldn't have come to this. Kate dear, could you look under your side plate please?"

Kade was puzzled but followed Emer's instructions. She lifted her side plate to find a yellowed old photograph underneath, which she examined with a confused expression.

"I don't understand," said Kade, holding up the picture for the others to see.

"Emer, please tell me you didn't?" Begged Sean as his face fell.

"It's just a little girl in a dress," said Kade, trying to figure out what the significance of the photo was.

"Look closer," Emer told her with a mischievous smile.

A sudden wave of realisation spread across Kade's face, which quickly turned to one of joy as she thrust the photograph in Sean's direction asking, "Is this you?"

"No. I mean yes, sort of," he stammered.

"In a dress?"

"It's not a dress, I was an Angel."

"In Heaven?"

"In the Nativity!"

Everyone around the table was now laughing except for Sean, who wished the ground would open up and swallow him.

"Busted!" Said Molly gleefully.

"You had such lovely blonde curls, where did they go?" Asked Kade.

"It was a long time ago," said Sean, reflexively running his hand through his hair.

"Check out the chubby knees, he still has those though," added Emer.

"Ha, ha, very funny. My knees are fine," Sean testily replied.

"Has he still got the fake wings?" Enquired Kade.

"He has, and the little halo. Would you not go home and get them for us Sean?" Teased Emer.

"Yes, let's play dress up!" Said Molly excitedly.

"I don't still have the wings," mumbled Sean.

"Aw, he's embarrassed, leave him alone," Kade replied, feigning sympathy for Sean's plight.

"You're right, we shouldn't be mean to him," conceded Emer.

"No we mustn't," said Kade, holding the picture up in front of her face while saying in a baby voice, "'Cause he's a widdle Angel."

Everyone laughed again and even Sean joined them this time, in spite of himself.

"Can you play the harp?" Asked Molly.

"No."

"Can we put you on top of our tree?" Said Patrick.

"No!"

"Can you grant wishes?" Added Kade.

"That's fairies. You're just being silly now."

It was too late for Sean though as the others teased him mercilessly the whole way through dinner, dessert, coffee and beyond.

Once the meal was over, Molly and Patrick went back to trimming the dining room Christmas tree while Sean and Kade helped clear the table. Emer gathered the last of the plates together before calling to the children, "Right you two, time to help with the dishes."

"But we're decorating the tree," they protested.

"I'm sure Sean and Kate won't mind finishing it off," Emer insisted.

"Just when I was getting to the good bit," grumbled Patrick with a fistful of tinsel in his hand.

"I'll put Christmas music on the kitchen TV, it'll be fun. Let's go."

Molly and Patrick reluctantly followed Emer to the kitchen leaving Sean and Kade to grab the discarded decorations and pick up where the kids had left off. They both worked in silence for a moment until Kade found something in the decorations box which she threw to Sean with a smile saying, "Here, catch."

Sean had his hands full of Lametta and just about managed to catch the object which, on closer inspection, turned out to be a decorative angel.

"Very funny," said Sean unimpressed.

"*I* thought so," replied Kade, tickled by her own joke.

"If you want to be helpful you can pass me some of that tinsel," he told her, pointing at the pile that Patrick had left behind.

Kade handed Sean a string of tinsel but, when he tried to pull it towards him, Kade held onto her end for a moment before letting go. It was a cute, flirty move which brought an involuntary smile to Sean's face.

"I'm sorry if I was mean to you about the photograph earlier," said Kade, now that the ice was broken.

"I guess I had it coming," admitted Sean, "I probably should have been nicer to you when you first arrived."

"Yeah, what was with that? Have you never spoken to a girl before?"

"I have, just not one as..." Sean began before catching himself just in time.

"As what?" Kade coyly asked.

"I was going to say as infuriating as you."

"Yeah, sure you were."

Kade gave Sean a meaningful look that made him blush but, before anything more could be said between them, they were interrupted by Molly, who came running into the room telling them both, "Come quick, I think you need to see this."

They both followed Molly into the kitchen to find Emer and Patrick watching a news report on the TV. Sean was unsure of what the big panic was about but Kade froze when she saw a photograph of herself superimposed on the screen as AJ interviewed Matty in the studio.

"Why is Kate on the TV?" Asked Molly.

"Hush," said Emer, turning up the volume while everyone else in the room watched the interview unfold in silent confusion.

"It must be great to have a number one box office movie but can you tell us what's happening with Kade?" Asked AJ, "She seems to have disappeared off the face of the earth."

"Well I'm in constant contact with her and she feels really bad about what happened at the concert," Matty replied, "Kade knows she let her fans down and that there's no excuse for it."

"Liar!" Kade furiously cried.

"So has she been miming this whole time?" Continued AJ.

"Pretty much," said Matty in that oily manner of his, "She claims to have lost her voice but the doctors can't find anything wrong with her, it's all just in her head."

"I've had enough of this," said Kade as she stormed angrily out of the room, followed quickly by Sean and Emer who were anxious to make sure that she was alright.

They found Kade on her phone in the hallway, trying unsuccessfully to get through to Marvin.

"Is there anything I can do to help?" Emer offered.

"No, I just need to go home," replied Kade as she redialled Marvin's number.

"Well it's dark, at least let Sean walk you back," suggested Emer.

"Not there, my home, my real home!" Snapped Kade.

Emer could understand why Kade was upset and so tried to comfort her guest by saying, "It's late, you should get some sleep, things will seem better in the morning."

"No they won't, I'm not going to sit around here in the middle of nowhere while some C list actor tears my whole life apart. I need to get out of this dump. Now!" Screamed Kade.

Sean and Emer were taken aback by the stinging ferocity of Kade's rebuke, especially since they were only trying to help.

"The nearest airport is hours away," said Emer, regaining her composure, "I'd take you myself but I have to cover the emergency clinic tonight."

"I'll drive," interrupted Sean, barely able to conceal the disdain he felt for Kade at that moment.

"Are you sure?" Asked Emer.

"Positive," Sean replied as he threw Kade a venomous look.

"I don't care who drives so long as I get out of here. I'm going to pack my things," said Kade, barging her way past them towards the door, leaving Sean to fume silently in her wake.

Chapter 6

Sean kept the engine running while he waited outside of White Rose Cottage for Kade to finish packing. He was furious at the way she'd spoken to his friend, especially after everything Emer had done for Kade since her arrival, but decided to hold his tongue as she'd be gone out of their lives forever in a few hours so why let some over indulged prima donna upset him any further.

For someone doing a moonlight flit, Kade was taking an awfully long time about it, eventually emerging from the cottage and dragging her luggage down the pathway. There were no bellhops around here, and Sean sure as hell wasn't going to help, but after a brief struggle, Kade managed to get her suitcases stowed in the car. Since the back seat was now full however she found herself having to sit in the front next to Sean, slamming the door as she got in so that he'd know she wasn't one bit impressed with this arrangement.

They drove off in a tense silence that barely lasted a mile before Sean could hold his peace no longer.

"You know that was really rude back there?" He said finally, trying his best to keep an even tone.

"Excuse me?"

"In Emer's house, you were insulting, condescending and you acted like a spoiled brat."

"How dare you, nobody speaks to me like that," said Kade, as her self-entitlement became further fuelled by righteous indignation.

"Well maybe it's time somebody did," Sean replied firmly.

"Why don't you just drive me to the airport and keep your opinions to yourself," Kade told him as she folded her arms in a snit.

Sean's angry retort would have to wait though as their conversation was interrupted by his phone suddenly ringing. He took the call on a Bluetooth earpiece he sometimes wore when there were passengers in the car so as to protect the privacy of his clients, not that Kade could give a damn about some Hicksville vet's telephone conversations. It didn't stop her being treated to a one sided conversation however which proved just as annoying.

"Hello?" Said Sean, listening intently to the other caller. "What, now? No, it's fine, I'll come straight away." His tone was urgent and if Kade hadn't picked up on the gravity of the situation from the way he spoke she was left in no doubt when Sean brought the car to a screeching halt and performed an emergency U-turn on the road.

"Wait, what are you doing?" She demanded.

"I've got a call out," said Sean, too busy executing the manoeuvre to look in her direction.

"You're supposed to be taking me to the airport, can't it wait?"

"It's an emergency."

"But I have a plane to catch," insisted Kade.

"The whole world doesn't revolve around you. It's about time you learned that," said Sean as he put the car into gear and sped off into the night.

※ ※ ※ ※ ※ ※

They hadn't been driving for more than ten minutes when Sean turned into a farmyard, bringing his car to a stop outside a large barn. He grabbed his medical bag from beneath Kade's luggage in the back seat and headed inside, with a barked instruction for her to, "Stay there."

This was like a red rag to a bull, prompting Kade to scramble out of the car after him insisting, "Don't you tell me what to do!"

Sean ignored Kade's protestations, which only made her angrier and so she followed him into the barn, determined not to let him have the last word.

Kade had her tirade locked and ready to go but was stopped in her tracks when she entered the barn to find Sean on his knees tending to a heavily pregnant cow that was lying on the straw.

As Sean carefully examined the cow's stomach Kade cautiously approached.

"Is she going to be alright?" Asked Kade, her anger now replaced by genuine concern.

"She's about to give birth but she needs a little help," advised Sean, "Can you pass me my bag?"

Kade duly brought Sean his bag and crouched down next to the cow, tenderly stroking its head while speaking in a soothing voice. "Don't worry sweetheart, everything's going to be just fine."

"You don't have to stay," said Sean, "The farmer will be back shortly."

"It's OK, I want to," replied Kade as, although she may have been the most self-centered person in the world when it came to humans, she could still empathise with an animal in distress.

"We could be here for a while," Sean warned her.

Kade looked into the cow's eyes and smiled, "I'll stay as long as it takes."

"I bet this is your first time in a barn," said Sean as he began to unpack the medical equipment from his bag.

Kade gave the place a once over before replying, "I did a music video in a barn once, but that was on a soundstage."

"Figures," smiled Sean to himself.

"Where are all the pigs and sheep?" Asked Kade, noticing the empty stalls.

"You're thinking of old McDonald."

"Shouldn't there at least be a camel?"

"That's the Nativity," replied Sean, barely able to hide his amusement.

"Well excuse me for not being an expert on barns, I'm a singer, not a farmer," said Kade with a hint of mock indignation in her voice. "I mean, I was a singer," she added quietly.

The awkwardness of the moment was interrupted by the cow suddenly crying out in pain.

"Well if you ever think of changing careers you're about to get your first lesson in being a midwife," said Sean, grabbing more supplies from his bag while Kade attempted to comfort the cow.

❈ ❈ ❈ ❈ ❈ ❈

The farmer returned from fetching fresh water to find Sean and Kade tending to a newborn calf while its mother looked sedately on. Kade turned excitedly to the farmer as he entered and announced, "It's a girl!"

"I can't thank you enough Sean," said the relieved farmer, dropping the buckets he was carrying to shake Sean's hand. "I thought I was going to lose her."

"All part of the service," Sean replied modestly.

"And you too nurse," continued the farmer to Kade.
"Oh, I'm not..." she began.

"I couldn't have done it without her," interrupted Sean.

"Well I'm grateful to you both. Will you stay for a cup of tea?" Asked the farmer.

"Thanks for the offer but I'm afraid we've got somewhere we need to be," said Sean as he grabbed his bag and headed for the door.

Kade dutifully followed him outside but this time her entrance into the car was much more subdued, accompanied by a distinct lack of door slamming.

"I can still drive you to the airport but you've probably missed the last flight," Sean told her as he started the car.

"It's fine, I'm tired anyway," replied Kade quietly. "Just take me back to the cottage for now and I'll try again in the morning."

Neither of them spoke on the journey home but Kade couldn't help but steal occasional glances across at Sean as there was something different about him now, something she hadn't noticed before. If only she could tell what that was.

As they came to a small pub that sat in darkness by the side of the road Sean pulled into the car park and turned off the engine.

"Why are we stopping?" Asked Kade.

"I meant what I said back there," Sean told her, "You really were a big help."

"It was nothing, really," Kade replied bashfully.

"Well the least I can do is buy you a drink to say thanks," said Sean as he opened the door to get out.

"What, here?" Asked Kade as she looked towards the darkened bar. "But the place is closed."

"This is Killarney," replied Sean with a mischievous look on his face, "The pubs are never really closed around here." With a wink and a grin he helped Kade out of the car and led her around to the side of the pub.

Sean gently knocked on a door that was barely visible from the road which, after a short wait, was opened a crack by a jolly red faced man in his 60s who whispered the greeting, "Tis yourself Sean, come on in, and you too miss, welcome."

Kade followed them both down a darkened hallway, the end of which opened out into a well-lit back lounge of the bar. She was surprised to find the place full of people but even more surprising was that Kade seemed to recognise most of the faces as the group were mainly composed of those who'd witnessed her initial arrival into the village on the back of Sean's cart.

Kade also spotted Bridget who was sitting by the fire talking to Father John.

As Sean and Kade made their way to the bar, people raised their glasses in muted welcome and while Sean ordered drinks Kade whispered to him, "Is it always so busy this late?"

"This is the best time of the night," replied Sean quietly, "The Guinness always tastes sweeter when you're not legally supposed to be drinking it."

He handed Kade a glass of stout and led her over to the fireplace to join his friends but Sean's greeting of "I'd like to introduce..." was interrupted by a smiling Father John admitting, "We've already met."

"Hi Kate," added Bridget, "I see you finally found some sensible footwear."

"A bit better for the country roads," Kade laughed.

Sean was so taken aback by their familiarity that he could only comment, "For someone who wasn't planning on sticking around you sure got your feet under the table with the locals."

"Maybe I'm not as shallow as you think," replied Kade.

"Well said," laughed Father John.

"Although I must say I'm surprised to see you here Father," continued Kade, "I didn't think you'd approve."

Father John responded by raising his glass in a toast saying, "Behold the rain which descends from heaven upon our vineyards. There it enters the roots of the vines to be changed into wine. A constant proof that God loves us and loves to see us happy."

"Is that a quote from the Bible?" Asked Kade.

"No," smiled the priest, "It's a quote from Benjamin Franklin."

"Well Amen to Ben," said Bridget as they all clinked glasses.

"So are you… *partaking*?" Kade diplomatically enquired as she gestured towards the drink in Father John's hand.

"No, this is just apple juice," he admitted, "A drop of communion wine on a Sunday is enough for me."

"The church is full of hypocrites," groused an inebriated Martin from his seat in the corner.

"Well there's always room for one more," quipped Father John.

The pub patrons found this hilarious, much to Martin's annoyance. His muttered response however was drowned out by Bridget scolding, "Oh shut up Martin!" before adding "Would somebody give us a song so we don't have to listen to that misery guts for the night."

There was a general murmur of agreement amongst the crowd which resulted in a guitar being produced from behind the bar.

As the drinkers began to good naturedly bicker over who would sing first, Bridget leaned in to Kade and whispered, "I see you've had a good evening."

"What do you mean?" Asked Kade, confused by the observation.

Bridget reached up and surreptitiously pulled a blade of straw from Kade's hair, causing her to blurt out, "It's not what you think," in flustered embarrassment.

"You don't have to explain to me, I was young once too you know," winked Bridget knowingly. "There's a toilet over there if you want to make sure there's no more *stray straw*."

Eager to avoid any further conversation on the subject, Kade slipped quietly away to the bathroom saying, "Maybe I'll just go wash my hands."

The ladies' bathroom consisted of one small cubicle so Kade was able to find privacy by locking the door behind her. This was her first time alone since the news report broke earlier that evening but when she turned on her phone she was surprised to find that there were still no messages or missed calls. Not from her celebrity friends, not from her management team and especially not from that so-called boyfriend of hers Matty. She was about to try Marvin's number again but thought better of it and put the phone away.

Instead, Kade examined her reflection in the mirror. Her hair was untidy but not messy, her woollen sweater was frayed but not ragged and she looked for all the world like a normal farm girl.

After washing her hands, Kade left the bathroom but when she returned to the bar she was surprised to see Sean playing the guitar while everyone listened in rapt silence.

Kade had never heard the song he was singing before but somehow it felt as familiar as one of her own, with its wistful air that spoke of love, longing and loss. When everyone in the bar joined in to sing the chorus, which urged a girl called Katie to come running home, it took all of Kade's will to hold back the tears. As if sensing her sadness Bridget gently squeezed Kade's hand to let her know she was among friends.

When the song finished, Sean passed the guitar to the next singer and re-joined the others by the fire, barely giving Kade enough time to regain her composure.

"Did you write that?" She asked.

"I wish," said Sean, "It's an old Irish song."

"It was beautiful."

Sean was too embarrassed by the unexpected compliment to reply, sensing that Kade would have pressed further were she not interrupted by a cry of, "Who's next for a song."

Her blood froze however when someone in the crowd suggested, "What about our friend from America?" Kade felt like a deer caught in the headlights when all eyes in the bar turned her way but a swift intercession by Father John rescued her as he told the others, "She's saving her voice for mass on Sunday, pick someone else."

People seemed to buy his explanation and moved on to a different singer, leaving a relieved Kade to mouth a silent 'Thank you,' to Father John who replied in kind by pretending to zip his mouth shut and lock it.

❊ ❊ ❊ ❊ ❊ ❊

The locals must have drank and sang for hours but to Kade, who had never felt this relaxed and happy around strangers in her whole life, the time seemed to fly by, so when the barman finally announced, "Right folks, it's time to finish up," she joined in with the chorus of complaints from the other patrons.

"Come on Frank, Martin is just starting to cheer up!" Bridget protested, as a now happy and animated Martin piped up, "Yeah Frank, don't be a misery guts."

"Alright, alright," grumbled the barman, "One more tune, but then that's it."

Bridget and Father John went to join the others in singing the last song, leaving Kade and Sean alone by the fire.

"You look tired," said Sean, noticing the heaviness in her eyelids.

"It's been a long night," Kade conceded.

"Maybe it's time to head back."

"Shouldn't we say goodbye?" Asked Kade in an uncharacteristically sociable manner.

"Do you want to be here for another hour?" Said Sean, nodding over at the raucous singers.

"I suppose not," Kade laughed.

"Don't worry, you'll see them all again," Sean replied. "Won't you?" He added questioningly.

Kade didn't answer, instead she quietly took her coat and slipped out of the seat towards the door.

Outside, the night had turned bitterly cold, forcing Sean and Kade to pull their collars up against the breeze as they made their way across the car park.

"How are we going to get back, we can't take the car," Kade asked, suddenly realising that they were in no fit state to drive.

"Don't worry," Sean assured her, "It's not too far, we can walk."

He went to lead them off down the road home but after a couple of steps Kade stopped. Noticing that she wasn't beside him anymore, Sean turned back and asked, "Is everything OK?"

"I just wanted to say thank you," Kade replied.

"For what?"

"For bringing me here tonight, I really enjoyed myself."

"You sound like you never had fun before," laughed Sean.

"Not like that I haven't," admitted Kade.

Sean was bemused by this and asked, "Like what?"

"Like the kind of fun that doesn't end up on the front page of a gossip magazine, or a TV news report."

Kade's words hung between them until the moment was broken by softly falling snow.

Taking off his scarf, Sean stepped forward and wrapped it around Kade's neck saying, "Here, we'd better get you bundled up."

As he fixed the scarf, Kade looked up at the falling snow and then down into Sean's eyes. "What a perfect way to end the evening," she whispered.

They moved slowly towards each other, as if about to kiss, but were interrupted by the pub door suddenly bursting open as the merry band of patrons were ushered out into the night.

"Come on Father, you of all people should know better," Frank complained, as Father John emerged, buttoning up his coat, followed by Bridget and the last few stragglers.

"All right Frank, cool your jets," laughed the priest.

Sean and Kade quickly parted and stood awkwardly next to each other as the crowd joined them in the snowy car park.

Noticing the guilty looks on both their faces, Bridget announced to no one in particular, "It's an awful shame to let the fun stop now," before roguishly adding, "I suppose we'll all just have to walk home, in the dark, *alone*," which prompted Kade to take a conspicuously large sidestep away from Sean.

Realising that if herself and Sean were left alone it would only complicate her life even more than it already was, Kade spoke up to suggest, "I suppose you could all come back to my place?"

The crowd cheered and on hearing Kade's offer, Frank nipped back into the pub, emerging with two crates of beer telling her, "Here, you can have these on the house for taking this lot off my hands."

"Well that settles it then. Sean, give the boys a hand," ordered Bridget, who'd made an executive decision to appoint herself the head (and sole member of) the party planning committee.

Bridget linked arms with Kade and led the others off down the snowy lane as the merry revellers serenaded them both with 'White Christmas,' much to Kade's amusement.

Chapter 7

In spite of the late hour, Kade's party was in full swing as everyone danced to the music coming from the pop video channel on the TV. She may not have been the most domestically gifted person in the world but if there was one thing Kade knew how to do it was throw a party and her little cottage was so full of people she was forced to squeeze through the crowd to reach Sean.

Handing him a beer, they shared a toast as Sean remarked, "So much for you being tired," to the now re-energised Kade.

"Like Bridget said, why let the fun end?" She told him.

"Are you sure that's the only reason you invited half of the village back?" He asked, raising his eyebrows.

"Of course," Kade replied coyly, "What other reason would there be?"

"I don't know," said Sean, "Maybe to avoid something? Or *someone?*"

Their conversation was interrupted by the crowd cheering as a party favourite song came on the TV.

"I love this tune!" Shouted Kade over the noise, pointedly using it as an excuse to slip away and join the other dancers.

Sean wasn't alone for long however as Bridget grabbed him by the arm and dragged him up dancing with the instruction, "Forget romance, just dance!"

Everyone in the cottage was now up on the floor but just as the dancers were getting into full swing, the song ended and when the next music video began the whole room froze, realising that it was one of Kade's most popular hits. They all turned towards her with worried looks on their faces, not knowing how she was going to react.

Kade stared mutely at the screen for a moment before loudly announcing to the room.

"Turn it up!"

As the partygoers cheered and began to dance again, Sean spotted Kade trying to slip out of the room unnoticed so he gently grabbed her arm and asked, "Can we talk?"

"Sure," she replied, "Just give me one minute though, there's something I need to do first."

Kade made her way into the empty kitchen but with the noise of the party still filtering in from the living room, she was forced to put her finger in one ear while she called Marvin's number, which rang three times before going to voicemail.

"This is Marvin, leave a message."

"Hey Marvin, I know you're screening your calls so I'll keep this short and sweet," she shouted over the racket, "You're fired!"

Hanging up with a satisfied look on her face, Kade returned to the party where she found Bridget dancing on the sofa as the crowd egged her on.

"Go Bridget! Go Bridget!" They chanted.

Becoming over excited from all the attention, Bridget tried to do the running man dance but instead fell backwards and disappeared down the back of the sofa.

Everyone rushed forward to help but before they could reach her, Bridget popped back up onto her feet, causing them to cheer, "Bridget!"

The crowd were jubilant but as Bridget waved her arms triumphantly above her head, Kade noticed that one of them was sticking out at a funny angle.

"Is your arm supposed to bend that way?" Kade asked in a concerned voice as everyone else in the room recoiled in horror.

"I'd better call the priest," said Sean, leaping into action.

"The priest?" Said a horrified Bridget. "To give me the last rites?"

"To drive you to the hospital, he's the only sober person in a twenty mile radius," replied Sean, dialling Father John's number while the women rushed to help the casualty.

❄ ❄ ❄ ❄ ❄ ❄

Bridget lay on a gurney in the Emergency Room with her arm in a plaster cast while Emer stood next to her in a white coat and scrubs, reading from a chart.

"It's just a small break, nothing too serious." Emer advised, "You're lucky Sean was there."

"Who, the vet?" Bridget grumbled, "I'm lucky alright, lucky he didn't shoot me."

"Well you're still alive, and if you want to stay that way you can give up dancing on sofas from now on," said Emer sternly.

"I can still dance though, can't I?"

"I've known you all my life Bridget, you could never dance. Now get some rest," Emer replied, closing the curtain around her bed before walking out into the corridor where Sean and Kade were anxiously waiting.

"Is she going to be alright?" Asked a worried looking Sean.

"Yes, no thanks to you. What were you thinking letting her carry on like that?" Emer chided.

"You shouldn't blame Sean, it was my idea to have a party," confessed Kade.

"It's not your fault, you're only new here. Sean knows better than to give Bridget too much booze," Emer explained. "Last Christmas she over indulged in the Sherry and the next morning we found her asleep in the manger cuddled up to the baby Jesus."

"I'm sorry," said Sean remorsefully, "Is there anything I can do to make amends?"

"Well you could start by taking piano lessons. Bridget is our only organist and she's supposed to be accompanying the choir on Christmas Eve," said Emer.

"But I haven't got a note in my head." Sean plaintively protested.

"I think I might know someone who could fill in at short notice," interrupted Father John as he returned from the vending machine carrying a tray of coffees.

"Someone local?" Asked Emer.

"Local enough," he replied, looking pointedly at Kade, who quickly stared down at her feet to avoid his gaze. "So how's the patient doing?" He enquired.

"She'll be fine," said Emer, "I'll keep her here for observation and drop her home when my shift ends."

"In that case I'd better get these two back," said Father John, "*Some of us* have to be up early for choir practice in the morning," he added, directing the comment towards Kade, who by now was sporting the guilty look of a bold child.

Chapter 8

White Rose Cottage's resident rooster crowed as the sun rose over its thatched roof later that same morning. Inside in the living room, the place was a complete mess, with empty bottles and party debris strewn everywhere. From under a bed cover on the sofa came the sound of a phone alarm insistently beeping until the blanket was finally thrown off by a fully dressed Kade, who had been sleeping underneath. She squinted at the time on her phone and groaned, turning off the alarm and sitting up in the process. Kade surveyed the mess for a moment but as she tried to stand up, the full effect of the previous night's debauchery hit her head on.

"Ow!" She cried, as a migraine kicked in at exactly the same moment her legs gave out. Falling back onto the sofa and closing her eyes, Kade promised herself, "Five more minutes."

The rooster however was having none of this and crowed again, which reverberated around the inside of Kade's head like a clap of thunder.

"Alright, alright, I'm coming!" She complained, while grabbing her coat and heading out the door, still in a bleary-eyed daze.

The overnight snow had carpeted the countryside, making the red and green colours of the holly and ivy bushes seem even more vibrant against the white backdrop. It was as if a Christmas card had come to life, complete with a red-breasted Robin that sat perched on the branch of a nearby tree, not that Kade noticed any of this as she huddled up inside her coat while walking the snow covered road towards the church.

Kade hadn't gone far however when she heard the sound of a car approaching from behind. As she stepped off the road to let it pass, Kade realised it was being driven by Emer, who pulled up and opened the passenger door saying, "Need a lift?"

"Badly," Kade replied gratefully as she got into the car, where Bridget was quietly snoring in the back seat.

"How is she?" Kade softly enquired, so as not to disturb the patient.

"About to wake up to the mother of all hangovers, but she'll survive," smiled Emer. "So where are you off to?"

"Church," Kade replied sullenly.

"You really do have a guilty conscience, don't you?" Said Emer in surprise.

"It's not that, I promised Father John I'd play the organ at choir practice to fill in for Bridget."

"Ah, I was wondering where he'd found an organist on such short notice."

"That's me, a regular old Liberace," Kade replied sarcastically.

"So playing the organ is your penance?"

Kade blinked away the sunlight reflecting off the snow and rubbed her tired eyes saying, "It sure is."

Emer let the conversation lull for a moment before continuing carefully, "So I suppose your secret is out?"

"I guess, the whole village must know who I am by now," said Kade quietly.

"Oh we always knew," Emer told her.

"You and the kids?"

"No, everyone."

"Everyone knew?" Said Kade, taken aback.

"You're one of the biggest pop stars in the world. I know we're a small bit detached from the outside world but it's Killarney, not the Kalahari."

"Why didn't anyone say something?"

Emer just shrugged her shoulders. "All that fame and fortune stuff isn't really important to people around here."

"Well I don't think the fame thing is going to be an issue much longer," Kade sighed.

"Anyway, that wasn't the secret I was talking about," Emer continued, "I meant your voice."

"Oh, that."

"Look, I'm not going to pry but I am a doctor so if you ever need someone to talk to?" Offered Emer.

"There's nothing to talk about. I've been to every vocal specialist in the world and they all say the same thing."

"Which is?"

"That there's nothing physically wrong with me. It's just down to stress. They say my voice could come back at any time."

"It's not unheard of," Emer admitted.

"I've been singing since I was a kid, it might seem like a glamorous life to others but for me it's just a treadmill," Kade told her, sounding as tired and defeated as the first day she'd arrived. "Touring and recording followed by more touring and more recording, I used to enjoy it but now? It's just a chore."

"Maybe a break would do you good?" Suggested Emer.

"I'm just a money making machine for people at this stage, they'll never let me stop."

"You need to do what's best for you, not for anyone else," said Emer as they pulled up outside the church.

"I'd better go," replied Kade as the weight of the conversation began to lay heavy on her.

"I have to drop Sleeping Beauty home but I'll pick you up on my way back," said Emer reassuringly. "Sometimes a nice cup of tea and a chat is the best medicine of all."

"Thanks, I'd like that."

Kade pulled her collar up around her as she walked the snow covered path to the chapel before pushing open the door and quietly slipping inside.

At the top of the church stood the choir, made up of the previous night's party guests, who were gathered around the organ looking the worse for wear. Father John was marshalling them into position when he spotted Kade and welcomed her by saying, "Right on time, have a seat, we're just about ready to begin."

Kade took her place at the organ but her co-ordination was still a bit hit and miss this early in the morning, so when she clumsily put her hands on the keys they produced a loud, discordant noise which didn't go down too well with the hungover choir.

"I'm sorry," apologised Kade, who was suffering the after effects of the party just as badly as they were.

Father John leaned over and turned the volume down on the organ saying, "Let's try that again, shall we?"

Kade regained her composure and began to play the opening bars of 'O Come All Ye Faithful'. When they got to the chorus however, Father John began to sing in a loud tenor voice, "O come all Ye faithful, joyful and triumphant!" Making Kade and the choir wince as the sheer volume of his voice aggravated their hangovers.

While Father John sang away with gusto, one of the choir members leaned over and whispered to Kade, "Could he not have picked Silent Night?"

This prompted Kade to secretly turn the organ volume down a couple of notches while the priest wasn't looking.

Father John wasn't kidding when he said the choir needed rehearsals and kept them there for nearly three hours until he'd gotten some semblance of a tune from them. When Kade and the other singers finally emerged wearily from the church she spotted Sean outside on the road beckoning her over.

"I thought Emer was collecting me?" She asked, joining Sean by his car.

"There's been a slight change of plan," he told her, "She sent me instead, hop in."

Kade got into the car and as Sean drove off asked, "Is everything all right?"

"No, well sort of," replied Sean, "You know how Emer's husband Liam is working abroad?"

"Yes, but he's due home in the next few days isn't he?"

"Well that's just it, there's a huge snowstorm heading his way so the airlines have started cancelling flights. With it being the holidays, everyone is scrambling to get out of there before the storm hits."

"You mean he won't be home for Christmas?" Kade gasped, "Patrick and Molly will be devastated."

"I wouldn't lose hope just yet. The airports are still open, for now," said Sean trying to stay positive. "It's just a case of finding him a seat. That's why Emer's not here, she's meeting with some travel agents in the city."

"Do you think he'll make it back in time?"

"It's touch and go, but never underestimate the magic of Christmas," smiled Sean hopefully as he pulled the car off the road and into a farmyard.

"Why are we stopping here?" Asked a puzzled Kade.

"Someone wants to say hello," replied Sean as he led Kade out of the car and into the barn.

Kade followed Sean inside where she found the cow from the previous evening waiting for them. Approaching softly, Kade asked her, "How's the new mommy doing?"

"Mother and baby are both doing fine," said Sean, as the newborn calf appeared from behind its mother and wobbled over to nuzzle Kade.

"Hello little lady, are you walking already?" Asked a delighted Kade, who laughed when the mother cow mooed in agreement.

"The farmer wants to call her Kate," said Sean.

"Such a pretty name for a pretty girl," replied Kade, gently stroking the calf.

"Or should that be Kade?" He added pointedly.

"Does it make a difference?" Asked Kade, unable to look Sean in the eye.

"Not to me," Sean told her.

"I prefer Kate."

"Then Kate it is," he said, nodding his assent.

"Emer said everybody knew who I was from the very start. Did you?" Asked Kade as she turned to face Sean.

"I had my suspicions," he replied honestly, "I mean, your clothes? Ladies around here wear more flannel than Chanel."

"So why didn't you say something?"

"I prefer to judge people by who they are rather than what they are. I was waiting until I got to know you better before jumping to any conclusions."

"But we didn't exactly get off to a great start."

"I had a feeling you'd come good in the end," smiled Sean.

"I'm not so sure about that," said Kade quietly.

"She seems to think so," replied Sean, as the calf reached up to lick Kade's hand.

"I wish I did."

Sensing Kade's sadness, Sean grabbed his bag and headed for the door telling her, "Come on, let's go," in a manner that suggested he wasn't going to take no for an answer.

"Go where?" She asked.

"I have something else to show you."

"More surprises?" Said Kade reluctantly.

"You'll like this one," promised Sean, as Kade climbed into the car beside him.

Chapter 9

Kade was relieved when Sean drove them the short distance back to White Rose Cottage. She was exhausted and the last thing she needed was to be dragged on some wild goose chase, however well-intentioned it may have been.

Sean wasn't letting her off that easily though and instructed Kade to, "Close your eyes," as they pulled up to the front of the cottage.

"Is this some kind of joke?" Sighed Kade, not able for any more of his shenanigans.

"It's not, trust me," Sean assured her.

Kade just closed her eyes and allowed Sean to lead her to the front door as it was easier than arguing with him.

"Ready?" Sean asked excitedly.

"No, but I don't think that's going to stop you," she replied.

Sean pushed open the front door of the cottage while gently guiding Kade inside. On opening her eyes, she was stunned to find that not only had all the party mess been tidied away but that Sean had also put Christmas decorations up around the living room, including a full sized tree.

Sean had one more surprise up his sleeve however and when he reached down behind the tree to turn the power socket on, the room was suddenly lit up by hundreds of fairy lights, which began to twinkle and flash, creating a magical atmosphere that took Kade's breath away.

"What do you think?" Asked Sean, pleased with his handiwork.

"It's the most beautiful thing I've ever seen," said an awestruck Kade.

"It's the best I could do on such short notice," he replied modestly.

Kade wandered over to take a closer look at the Christmas tree and was amazed to find that Sean had hung porcelain white rose decorations on the branches.

"Where did you get these?" Said Kade as she gently examined the ornaments.

"Well, since the place is called White Rose Cottage I thought it would be nice to put some on the tree, do you like them?" Sean asked.

"They're perfect," she replied emotionally.

One of Kade's earliest memories was her dad buying her mom white roses every year on their anniversary. Sadly they'd both passed away before Kade had become famous and so she always surrounded herself with white roses as a way to remember them by. It was a secret she'd never shared with anyone else in her life, not even Marvin, but to see them here now on this tree meant the world to Kade.

In that moment Sean could see the look of a lost little girl on Kade's face and so he pulled one of the giant backed comfortable armchairs up to the roaring log fire and offered, "Here, take a seat."

Kade settled back into the chair and as she closed her eyes the comforting heat from the fire felt like a hug from loved ones long gone.

Disappearing into the kitchen, Sean returned with two steaming mugs, handing one of them to Kade.

"What is this?" She asked as the aroma of hot spices drifted up from the mug.

"Mulled wine," Sean replied, "It's been cooking on the stove."

Kade took a deep, satisfying draught from her mug before asking, "Did you put all of these decorations up by yourself?"

"No," laughed Sean, "Martin helped, he can be a cheery little elf when he wants to. It's the least we could do, especially after the mess we made with the party."

"You didn't have to go to all that trouble," said Kade gratefully.

"I know," he replied, "I wanted to."

As if to further prove his contrition, Sean opened a cupboard in the corner of the room to reveal a set of neatly stacked suitcases. "I even tidied your luggage away," he said proudly.

"You think of everything," she smiled.

Sean sat in the armchair opposite Kade and, reaching down beside his seat, produced a Christmas cracker which he presented to her.

"What's this?" She asked while quizzically examining the cardboard paper tube that had been wrapped in brightly coloured paper and twisted at both ends.

"It's a Christmas cracker," said Sean, not realising that crackers were one of those Christmas traditions that hadn't made their way back across the Atlantic.

"I'm supposed to eat this?" Asked a naturally confused Kade.

"No, you're supposed to pull it, let me show you," Sean replied as he reached across to grab one end of the cracker.

Kade cautiously pulled the other end which tore apart with a bang, causing her to fall backwards on the chair with surprise as Sean laughed.

"Is this another one of your tricks?" She fumed with mild annoyance.

"No, have you never seen a Christmas cracker before? Look inside."

Kade emptied the contents of the cracker onto her hand, which consisted of a heart shaped key ring, a paper crown and a piece of paper that she read aloud.

"What did one snowman say to the other?"

"I don't know," replied Sean, "What did one snowman say to the other?"

"Are your hands sticky?"

Sean thought this was hilarious but Kade was confused, "I don't get it," she told him, not sure if it was supposed to be a riddle or a joke.

"Because the snowman's hands are made of sticks?" Sean explained, as if the punchline's meaning was patently obvious.

Kade just stared at him blankly prompting Sean to reply, "Oh just put your hat on," in a jovially dismissive tone.

To keep him quiet, Kade placed the paper hat on her head and sat back into the chair with her mulled wine.

"And there she is, the queen of Christmas," Sean announced cheerily.

"Yeah, Christmas," Kade replied, looking thoughtfully into the fire.

"So is this what your house looks like on the holidays?" Sean enquired.

"Which one, I have five."

"Whichever one you call home."

"I'm hardly ever in one long enough to call it home," Kade told him. "Most of my life is spent in hotel rooms, including at Christmas."

"So where are you going to spend this one?" Sean asked leadingly.

"Well, since I've promised Father John that I'll play the organ at midnight mass on Christmas Eve, I guess I'm stuck here."

"There are worse places you could be," said Sean, sounding a little hurt.

"I'm sorry, I didn't mean it like that," apologised Kade.

"It's fine, let me get you a refill," he replied, taking Kade's mug and heading to the kitchen.

"I'll help," Kade told him and got up to follow.

As Sean ladled the mulled wine into the mugs, Kade leaned in over him to have a look at the spices floating in the pot, a move which inadvertently brought them as close together as they had been on that night in front of the pub.

"Thanks again for doing all of this," she told him, "It's been a long time since I've felt Christmassy."

"You're welcome," smiled Sean, happy to see her softer side coming out.

They toasted each other while sharing a look that was only broken by Sean asking, "So, since you're staying in Killarney for Christmas will you be cooking your own turkey?"

"Me? Cook?" Said Kade, laughing at the very notion. "I used to make toast but I lost the recipe."

"You could have Christmas dinner at my place?" Sean casually offered.

"Oh, I don't think that would be a good idea," Kade answered reluctantly.

"Why not?" He continued, "Everyone else is coming, Emer, Liam, the kids."

"Well, in that case," Kade quickly replied, suddenly not so hesitant now that she'd realised it hadn't been an invitation to a dinner for two.

"Did you think I was asking you out on a date?" Sean laughed.

"No," Kade replied defensively.

"Don't worry, I'm not that forward," he smiled, "I'm an old-fashioned guy, I prefer to woo a girl."

That last part caused Kade to almost choke on her mulled wine. "*Woo?*" She questioned laughingly.

"Yes, woo."

"As in?"

"As in, Woooo!" Sean replied, making a spooky sound.

"What's that supposed to be?"

"The ghost of Christmas future?" He coyly smiled.

They gazed at each other for a moment until Sean broke the tension by grabbing his coat and announcing, "That settles it then."

"Where are you going?" Asked Kade, worried that his sudden departure had been caused by something she'd said.

"Well if I'm going to have an extra guest for Christmas dinner then I'll obviously need to get more food won't I?"

Of course he was right but this guy sure knew how to keep a girl off balance, thought Kade as she drained her glass to recover from their moment.

"And more wine too by the look of it," added Sean as he watched her empty the mug in one go.

"Hey!" Protested Kade in mock indignation.

"I won't be long," Sean told her as he headed for the door, "Why not take it easy until I get back."

Kade looked around at the decorations, the twinkling lights on the tree, the roaring log fire and said "Thanks, I will."

She meant it too, at that moment in time there was nowhere else in the world she'd rather be.

Sean had been gone less than a minute but startled Kade by suddenly rushing back in through the front door. "Sorry, forgot my car keys," he said apologetically before departing again and closing the door behind him.

To get over her surprise, Kade treated herself to another mug of mulled wine from the pot before making her way back to the armchair by the fire. She had barely sat down however when a knock came to the door, which she got up to answer while complaining, "What have you forgotten this time scatterbrain?" Upon opening it however, Kade was stunned to find Marvin standing on her doorstep.

"How's my favourite superstar?" He said brashly, kissing Kade on both cheeks before barging past her into the cottage. Marvin briefly surveyed the sitting room with a condescending look before turning to Kade and asking, "Who decorated this place, the Keebler elves?"

"What are you doing here Marvin?" Kade demanded, having recovered from her initial shock.

"What do you think I'm doing here? I've come to take you home."

"Take me home? I've been calling you non-stop day and night and you couldn't even be bothered to answer your phone."

"I was busy trying to save your career," said Marvin indignantly.

"Well in case you didn't get the message I left you then I'll tell you in person. I quit!" Kade told him in no uncertain terms.

"Quit? You're a superstar, superstars don't quit." Marvin replied dismissively.

"Well I just did."

"You're upset, I get that," said Marvin in that smarmy voice of his. "But I have something here that will cheer you up," he continued, opening a video message on his phone and handing it to Kade.

The message was a recording of Matty, who was holding an enormous bunch of red roses. "Hey babe, I miss you so much," he began, "Can't wait to have you back in my arms so we can spend Christmas together."

"See?" Said Marvin, as if this was somehow supposed to make everything alright.

"See what?" Snapped Kade, slamming the phone back at Marvin. "He threw me under the bus on live TV just to promote his dumb movie."

"Kade, babe, it's not like that," said Marvin trying to affect a conciliatory tone. "He was doing it for you, it was all part of the plan."

"Plan? What plan?" She demanded.

"To win people over by playing the sympathy card, and it worked like a charm. The whole world feels sorry for you, they share your pain."

"The only pain I have right now is you Marvin," Kade fumed.

"Don't you get it? Everybody loves a comeback story," he continued undeterred. "We're flooded with offers for book deals, TV appearances, they even want to make a movie of the week about you."

"So I'm supposed to just drop everything and go running back, is that it?" Asked Kade sarcastically.

Marvin looked around the room and sneered, "Drop what, this?"

"I made promises!" Kade insisted.

"Promises to who?" Said Marvin, his tone becoming more domineering. "This is just some fantasy, a temporary escape. It's time to go back to the real world."

Kade began to waver, maybe it was the shock of seeing Marvin, or the fact that deep down she knew he was telling the truth, but her emotions were in turmoil as she replied "I don't know, I need time to think."

"We don't have time," continued Marvin, now piling on the pressure. "There's a private jet waiting for us at the airstrip. You have a once in a lifetime chance to get back everything you've lost and more. Don't blow this again Kade, we need to go, and we need to go now!"

Torn between two worlds, Kade looked around the cottage and then back at Marvin.

Chapter 10

Sean was in high spirits as he drove back from town with the Christmas supplies. Pulling up outside the cottage, he took the shopping bags from the car, awkwardly transferring them all onto one hand so he could fish out his keys. When he reached the door however, Sean found it ajar and so he pushed it open and walked cautiously inside.

"Kate? Are you here?" He called, setting the bags on the floor.

The house was silent but when Sean went to the kitchen to look for Kade, he instead found a folded piece of paper on the counter with his name written on the front. Opening the page Sean read the two word note that simply said 'I'm sorry.'

Rushing back into the living room in a confused panic, Sean wrenched open the cupboard door only to have his worst fears confirmed as all of Kade's suitcases were now gone. He ran outside, hoping beyond hope that this was some sort of prank but Kade was nowhere to be seen.

Over by the crossroads, Father John was busy setting up the Nativity scene outside the church when a black sedan with tinted windows sped past. The car obviously didn't belong to anyone local but he blessed himself regardless as someone travelling at that speed would need all the grace they could get.

Back at the cottage, Sean was still in a daze but seeing Kade's half empty mug sitting by the fireplace brought him suddenly back to his senses and so, quickly grabbing his keys, Sean raced back outside and jumped in his car.

At the local pub, the barman was sweeping his front step when the black sedan shot past. On some mercy dash no doubt to be travelling at such speed, he thought to himself.

By now Sean had reached the crossroads and was frantically looking for a clue as to which direction Kade had gone. Spotting Sean's obvious distress, Father John approached the car to ask, "Is everything alright?"

"You didn't see anyone pass this way?" Sean asked desperately.

"There was a black car came by here just a few minutes ago," Father John told him, "It was heading towards town but…"

"Thanks Father," interrupted Sean, speeding off before the poor priest could even finish his sentence.

As the sedan passed through the village on its way to the airfield, Kade looked mournfully out the window, hoping to catch one last glimpse of a friendly face. Marvin on the other hand was in decidedly better spirits, having gotten his money spinner back, and as they neared their destination he cheerfully whistled 'Take me Home, Country Roads'.

Back at the pub, the barman was pointing Sean in the direction of the village as he took off again in pursuit of Kade.

The private jet sat idling on the runway as the sedan arrived, with Marvin quickly bundling Kade aboard before she could even snatch a last look at what had been her adopted home.

As the engines revved up, Sean was speeding his way out of the village, having been directed towards the airstrip by the locals, who'd realised that something was afoot.

With their final pre-flight checks completed, the pilots gunned the engines, sending the jet hurtling down the runway and skyward. As the plane took off, it passed over the approach road at the very moment Sean was arriving.

Bringing the car to a screeching halt, Sean jumped out and began waving his arms in a last-ditch effort to attract Kade's attention, sadly though the plane was travelling too fast for him to be noticed and so he was forced to watch in helpless despair as it disappeared into the sky.

When the plane finally broke through the clouds, Kade gazed forlornly out the window at the setting sun.

"Cheer up," commented Marvin from the adjacent row of seats, "At least you'll be home for Christmas."

Chapter 11

It had been days since Kade left but, despite scouring the internet, Sean was unable to find a single mention of her whereabouts no matter how hard he looked. It was as if she'd just disappeared into thin air. In the end Sean gave up looking as the constant searching was only making things harder for him. He needed to face up to the fact that what had happened between him and Kade wasn't real, world famous celebrities didn't fall for ordinary guys in real life, that kind of thing only happened in the movies. "This isn't Notting Hill," he kept telling himself.

To take his mind off of things, Sean threw himself into his work, it wasn't as if things weren't busy at this time of the year anyway, especially not when he was the only vet for miles around. In spite of the workload however, Sean also volunteered his evenings to help get the church ready for Christmas Eve and whatever spare minute he had after that was spent working on the farm, anything to keep his mind off the events of the past few weeks.

The one consolation for Sean was that the farmyard chores he'd been putting on the long finger for months, or even years, were finally getting done, one of which was cleaning out the shed so that his donkey would have a place to stay for the winter.

As Sean dragged the old brass bed out from the wall he discovered a tag off one of Kade's suitcases that had fallen down the side on the first night she'd stayed there. The mere sight of this seemingly innocuous luggage accessory brought a wave of memories and emotions flooding back which would have overwhelmed Sean were it not for the interruption of a car pulling up on the road outside and beeping its horn.

Sean dropped the tag and rushed expectantly outside, hoping that it signalled Kade's return, but the disappointment on his face was clearly obvious when he realised that it was only Father John, who greeted him with a sympathetic, "Morning Sean, heard anything?"

"Nothing," said Sean, dejectedly shaking his head.

"I'm sorry," consoled Father John, empathising with Sean's sense of loss.

Sean just shrugged his shoulders and with an air of resignation replied, "What's the point of feeling sorry for myself when there are people with bigger problems?"

"Emer and Liam," nodded Father John gravely, "How's it looking?"

"Not too good, he's still stuck at the airport," said Sean, "It seems the storm is due to hit soon so all the remaining flights are completely booked out."

"Could he not drive back?" Asked Father Sean hopefully.

"It's Christmas Eve, he'd never make it home in time."

"The kids will be heartbroken," sighed Father John.

"I know," agreed Sean, and what more could be said.

"I'm on my way there now if you want a lift?" Father John offered.

"Sure," said Sean, glad of an excuse to get away from the memories that this place still held. Joining Father John in the car, they continued on to Emer's house.

❋ ❋ ❋ ❋ ❋ ❋

Parking the car on the road at the back of the house, Father John and Sean entered through the kitchen door where they found Emer sitting at the table, anxiously typing on her laptop.

"Oh, hi," she said absentmindedly, barely looking up from the screen. "There's tea in the pot."

"We're fine, thanks. What are you up to?" Asked a worried Sean. Emer was the most together person he knew and to see her like this had him concerned.

"I've been scouring all the booking sites trying to find a last minute cancellation," she replied, "I even messaged everyone in my contact list to see if they could help."

"Any luck?"

"Nothing," sighed Emer, still typing away in the vain hope of finding a flight home for her husband.

"I've been praying for a miracle," Father John added.

"I know you have," said Emer gratefully, "It means a lot."

Sean poked his head into the living room where Patrick and Molly were staring blankly at a Christmas movie on the TV.

"Hi kids," he said, forcing a cheery note into his voice, but neither of them answered, just quietly waving an acknowledgement instead.

Deciding to leave them be for now, Sean went back to the kitchen where Emer was bringing Father John up to speed on the latest developments.

"I told Liam I'd ring him at eleven," she explained as the clock on the wall was just coming up to the hour.

"Well don't mind us, you go ahead," Father John told her.

Emer didn't bother leaving the room to make the call, as Sean and Father John were practically family, and she wanted them close by for moral support in case Liam had bad news for her.

Emer dialled Liam's number but immediately got a 'your call cannot be connected' message.

"Here let me try," offered Sean as he took out his phone and began to dial.

Father John couldn't hear the other end of the call but could tell by the way Sean's face fell that he too had gotten the same recorded message.

"Anything?" Emer asked hopefully, even though in her heart of hearts she already knew the answer.

"No connection," Sean replied quietly, "The storm must have knocked out the phones."

"So that's it then," said Emer as she buried her head in her hands.

As Father John went to console her a knock came to the front door.

"I'll get it," said Sean. in an effort to make himself feel useful.

He went out to the hall and opened the front door, expecting to find one of the neighbours calling to offer comfort, but instead was stunned to discover Liam standing there with suitcases in hand and a smile as broad as the Shannon on his face.

"Liam?!?" Sean exclaimed in shock.

His cry of surprise caused a sudden commotion from inside the house as everyone came running to the hallway.

"Liam?" Said Emer incredulously, not able to believe her eyes.

"Daddy!" Cried Molly and Patrick, running down the hallway and jumping into their father's arms.

The house became a flurry of activity as the children led Liam into the kitchen while Sean and Emer followed, still in a state of shock. Out in the hallway, Father John brought his hands together, raised his eyes and offered up a silent prayer of gratitude.

"I can't believe you made it back," Emer told her husband when she finally found enough room in between the kids to give him a hug.

"You and me both," said Liam, sounding relieved to be home.

"But how?" She asked, still not able to take it all in.

"It was the craziest thing," Liam began, "We were sitting in the airport watching the storm approaching when suddenly my name was called out over the intercom telling me to go to the information desk. I thought it might have been you trying to contact me but when I got there they rushed me down to the runway where, and this is the wildest part, there was a private jet waiting."

"A private jet?" Cried Emer and Sean simultaneously.

"I know, right?" Liam continued, "At first I thought it was a mistake but they said it was definitely for me."

Sean didn't wait to hear the rest, he ran back to the front door and pulled it open, hoping to find Kade's black sedan waiting outside. Instead, all he saw was a local taxi pulling away onto the road after having dropped Liam off from the airport.

In all of the troubles he'd encountered throughout his life, Sean had never felt his heart sink as fast as it did in that moment, it was like losing Kade all over again.

Sean wanted nothing more than to go home and curl up in a ball but his friends were here and right now they needed him, so he put on a brave face and returned to the kitchen where Liam was still recounting his tale.

"I mean, who do we know with a private jet?" Liam asked the others.

Everyone turned to look sympathetically at Sean who just bowed his head quietly.

"Am I missing something?" Said Liam, sensing the sudden change in mood.

"I'll tell you later," Emer discreetly whispered.

"I need to go," announced Sean, feeling a sudden urge to be alone.

"I understand," said Father John, putting a consoling hand on his shoulder. "Will we see you this evening for mass?"

"I'll be there," nodded Sean, knowing that however bad he felt now, missing the Christmas Eve service would only make him feel worse.

"And don't worry about Christmas dinner, we can have it here instead," Emer offered, "I'll cook."

"Thanks," replied Sean, cutting a forlorn figure as he made his way out the back door, leaving the others to fill Liam in on the whole sorry saga.

Chapter 12

It was a clear, moonlit night and although more snow had been forecast there was no sign yet of its arrival. The blanket of white left over from the last flurry however was enough to make it a picture-perfect Christmas Eve. Outside of the village church, the parishioners were adding some final flourishes to the crib while inside the choir were gathered on the altar for a last rehearsal, as Bridget attempted to play the organ with her one good hand.

"I think I can manage," she told the others, but the faces the choir were making in response to her attempts said otherwise.

"We're probably better off doing without the organ this year," said Father John tactfully.

"But it's tradition," protested Bridget.

"Then we'll start a new one," he replied softly, aware of how badly Bridget felt.

"This is all my fault," she said, ruefully looking down at the cast on her arm.

"It's no one's fault," Father John insisted, knowing that Christmas was a time for love and forgiveness, not guilt and recriminations.

Back at the bungalow, Emer and Liam were helping Molly and Patrick on with their coats.

"Ready?" Asked their mother.

"All set," said Patrick, before excitedly opening the door and rushing off down the path with Molly.

Emer linked arms with Liam and they followed the children up the snowy road to the church.

As they passed the farm, they ran into Sean, who had just finished bedding his animals down for the night.

"How are you feeling?" Asked Emer sympathetically.

"I've been better," admitted Sean with an air of defeat in his voice.

"At least you still have us," Emer replied, giving him a comforting hug.

"Thanks," said Sean, grateful for the support of his friends at a time like this.

Emer took Molly and Patrick by the hands and led them on ahead, giving Sean and Liam a chance to talk in private.

"Emer's been filling me in on everything that's happened," began Liam, "It sounds unbelievable."

"That's one way to describe it," said Sean, in little humour to relive the recent past.

"I mean, some world famous superstar showing up in a place like this? I thought things like that only happened in the movies," Liam continued, echoing Sean's own sentiments.

"At least movies have a happy ending," Sean answered, the sadness clearly etched on his face.

"So you really liked her? This singer?" Liam asked.

"I thought I did," shrugged Sean.

"Then would you not try to follow her back to America?"

"What's the point?" Sean replied, "Even if I could find her it would never work between us. It's like you said, she's a world famous superstar and I'm just a vet, living alone out here in the middle of nowhere."

"Don't sell yourself short," insisted Liam.

"I'm not, I'm just being realistic."

"Give it time. I'm sure you'll meet a nice girl someday."

"Around here?" Said Sean sceptically as he gestured to the empty fields surrounding them.

"Have you thought of going back to your old job?" Liam suggested, "You'd surely have a better chance of finding someone in the city"

"No," replied Sean with an air of regret in his voice, "Whatever little there is for me here, there's even less there."

It broke Liam's heart to see his best friend like this, especially after everything that he'd done for Emer and the kids over the past few weeks, which is why he was determined not to let Sean wallow in his own misery.

"You need to stay positive," Liam told him, "Look at me, I wouldn't have my family if it wasn't for you introducing me to Emer."

"You got lucky," replied Sean.

"And you will too, you just have to believe."

"There's no pot of gold at the end of my rainbow," sighed Sean, "I've made my peace with that."

Realising there was little more he could say, Liam just put a supportive arm around his friend as they caught up with Emer and the kids.

❋ ❋ ❋ ❋ ❋ ❋

The closer they got to the church, the more people joined them on the road, each one sharing gestures of sympathy with Sean while they walked to midnight mass together.

Once inside, the congregation took their seats as Father John welcomed them warmly from the altar.

"Good evening everyone," he began.

"Good evening Father," they replied in unison.

"You're all very welcome here to the most special night of the year."

Father John's introduction was suddenly interrupted by the wind blowing open the door to reveal a figure standing in the darkened archway. Startled by the commotion, everyone turned expectantly towards the back of the church, but as the figure stepped into the light they were disappointed to see that it was only Martin.

"Oh come in Martin!" Shouted Bridget from somewhere near the top of the chapel.

All eyes turned back to Sean who simply bowed his head in defeat. It seemed that he wasn't the only one who had been hoping for a Christmas miracle and now the others too shared in his sadness.

Sean spent the rest of the service in a world of his own, oblivious to everything but the thoughts of his loss, and it was only when mass was nearing its end did he come back to the real world.

Father John walked to the front of the altar to address the congregation. "We've reached that time of the evening where we celebrate the lighting of the candles," he told them, "As is the tradition..."

The priest suddenly stopped mid-sentence, clearly taken aback by something at the rear of the chapel. The crowd followed his gaze, unsure of what had caused him to lose his train of thought, to find that Kade had just slipped quietly through the door and was now nervously staring back at the throng of expectant faces looking in her direction.

Her natural instinct was to just turn around and run back out the way she'd come in, but before Kade could come to a decision, Father John beckoned her forward encouragingly.

Keeping her head bowed, Kade made her way up the aisle, too embarrassed to make eye contact with anyone, especially not Sean. When she reached the organ, Kade sat down and whispered an apologetic, "Sorry I couldn't be here sooner," to Father John, who replied, "Better late than never," before picking up where he left off.

"As I was saying," he continued, "We're now going to have the traditional lighting of the candles so if all the children can come forward?"

The lights in the church dimmed to near darkness while the children collected their tapers and began to slowly make their way around the church, bringing to life the rows of candles on the votive stands that lined the aisles. As the glow of the candles illuminated the chapel the choir began to sing, this time accompanied by Kade on the organ.

The sight of the church lit by candlelight was breathtaking, especially for Sean who sat captivated by the sight of Kade as she played with all her heart.

When the choir finished singing, Father John returned to the altar and brought the ceremony to a close by telling the congregation, "Thank you for being here to celebrate this wonderful evening, where you can all agree that we've seen the magic of Christmas first hand."

All eyes in the church were now on Sean and Kade.

"So let us go in peace and love," continued Father John, before adding, "And hurry home because Santa is on his way!" Much to the delight of the children.

As the mass ended, everyone stood up to exchange final farewells with their families and friends while Kade made use of the distraction to grab her coat and slip quietly out the side door unnoticed. She had only managed to make it half way down the path however when Sean came rushing out of the church after her.

"Wait!" He called.

Too ashamed to face him, Kade kept walking until Sean caught up and gently turned her around.

"Were you just going to leave again without saying a word?" He asked, confused by Kade's reluctance to stay behind.

"I didn't want to cause any trouble," she told him, unable to meet Sean's gaze.

"It's a bit late for that," he replied, not meaning it to sound as harsh as it did.

"I'm sorry for everything that's happened," said Kade, "I wanted to apologise to you in person, I really did."

"And then what, just disappear off into the night again?" Sean demanded. "I can't get my heart broken twice Kate."

"It's Kade."

Sean stepped closer to her now saying, "No it isn't. Kade is a face on the TV, a voice on the radio. That's just a part you play, Kate is the real you."

Kade turned to walk away, her eyes welling up as she told Sean, "This was a mistake. I shouldn't have come here."

"Then why did you?" He called after her.

Kade stopped for a moment and without turning explained, "I thought that if I saw you in person I'd be able to say a proper goodbye, but I can't."

"Why not?"

"Because I never want to say goodbye to you," Kade replied, unable to hold back the tears any longer.

"Then don't," said Sean softly.

That was all Kade had ever wanted to hear and so, turning back towards Sean, she rushed into his arms, kissing him as the first flurries of snow began to swirl around them.

Sean held Kade in an embrace that she hoped would never end, a wish that wasn't to be however as their magical moment was interrupted by the sound of someone behind them clearing their throat.

"Ahem," came the voice.

Sean and Kade turned to find that the whole congregation had now come outside and were staring at them in amazement, including a bemused Father John who was holding a statue of the baby Jesus in his arms while covering its eyes with one hand to preserve the infant's innocence.

"Oh!" Said a startled Kade.

"I don't mean to interrupt you but we need to put this little fella to bed," Father John smiled.

Sean and Kade shared an embarrassed laugh as everybody gathered around them at the manger, with Emer and Liam having to push their way through the crowd to reach their friends as Molly and Patrick rushed forward to hug Kade.

"Thank you so much for bringing our daddy home," they told her.

"You saved our Christmas," added Emer, "But how did you know?"

"You sent a message to all your contacts asking for help," Kade revealed, "You must have forgotten that my number was still in your phone."

"And here I was thinking that you had psychic powers," laughed Emer, "I can't thank you enough."

"It was nothing," Kade humbly replied.

"It wasn't nothing, it was everything," said Emer, "I can't believe you came back."

"What can I say," answered Kade emotionally, "Killarney called me home."

As Emer and Kade hugged, Father John moved towards the manger to finish the Nativity ceremony. The congregation fell silent but just as he was about to put the baby Jesus in the crib a voice in the crowd began to sing.

Turning to see where such a beautiful sound was coming from, the parishioners were shocked to discover that it was in fact Kade.

"Silent night, holy night,
All is calm and all is bright," she sang.

Sean put his arm around her for support as the congregation joined in the chorus,

"Round yon virgin, mother and child,
Holy infant, so tender and mild,
Sleep in heavenly peace,

Sleep in heavenly peace."

Epilogue

Kade was woken early the following morning by Molly jumping on her bed and excitedly shouting "Wake up, it's Christmas!" Judging by the noise coming from the room next door, it sounded like Sean was getting the same treatment from Patrick. Emer had insisted they sleep over so that everyone could open their presents together and Kade wouldn't have missed spending Christmas with a real family for anything in the world. She put on her robe and joined the others in the living room where the kids were excitedly opening their presents. Emer had made sure that nobody was left out and handed Kade and Sean a gift each. They laughed as Kade unwrapped her 'Cooking for Beginners' book while Sean opened his 'Playing the Organ for Dummies'.

The rest of the day was a whirlwind of activity, in the kitchen Sean prepared dinner while Kade watched on from behind as she leafed through her cookery book in bewilderment. Things got even more hectic when Bridget and Father John arrived, carrying armfuls of presents, and the kids thought it hilarious when Bridget insisted that Kade sign her cast.

The dinner was a triumph and everyone cheered as Kade and Sean brought in the turkey and ham. They cheered even louder when Kade pulled a cracker with Father John and got startled by its bang for a second time. It was a Christmas day to remember and while the adults and children slept off their big meal in front of the TV, the dirty dishes went ignored in the sink as Kade and Sean sneaked into the back yard to kiss under the mistletoe tree while a donkey looked on over the hedge.

The End

Author's Note

Due to copyright reasons, I was unable to print the lyrics of the song Sean sang to Kade in the pub but it can be found by searching for 'Mary Black - Katie' in your preferred music provider. To those of you curious about the cryptic dedication at the start of the book, I highly recommend you watch the holiday movie 'A Wonderful Christmas Time' (2014) by Jamie Adams to learn more.

I'm currently working on my next book 'Emily', a John Hughes style romantic comedy set in the 1980's, so for more information on this and further titles in the Holiday Novella series you can find me on Twitter @CarrieClane. Thank you so much for reading this book and whichever way you choose to celebrate the season I hope you all have a happy and safe one.

Nollaig Shona Daoibh.

Carrie